CW00859074

DARUMA'S SECRET

Neil Frankland

authorHOUSE®

AuthorHouse™ UK Ltd.
500 Avebury Boulevard
Central Milton Keynes, MK9 2BE
www.authorhouse.co.uk
Phone: 08001974150

First published by AuthorHouse 4/14/2009

ISBN: 978-1-4389-7004-2 (sc)

Printed in the United States of America
Bloomington, Indiana

This book is printed on acid-free paper.

Dedicated to Oliver and Sarah,

You have provided the inspiration and the motivation,
All my love

Neil

Acknowledgements

There are a few people who I wish to thank for helping me write this story. Some of you will know me but others will not even realise that they have been influences.

For those that know me, Sarah and Oliver have kept me going through hard times. I haven't always being the most conventional Husband or Father but that's the way I am, I've always done things in a topsy-turvy sort of way. That kind of sums up our relationship really!

Thank you Darin Jewell, my agent, for having faith in me and what I write. I'm glad you represent me and that you have the patience to guide me in this. I know I haven't been the easiest of people, probably due to my naivety, but I'm just happy to know we are getting this off the ground.

Jenna Atkinson at TGI Fridays has been a revelation in finding someone with the same ambition as myself and being able to sound off about writers block or how do I convey this message or that. It's refreshing to know that someone understands my reasons for doing this and has backed and encouraged me all the way.

Patrick McCarthy has provided information about the Bubishi that only he can provide. He will not realise that he has inspired me but he has. I have read his book on the Bubishi and it has left a lasting impression. Victor Smith's articles on Fighting Arts. com have also done a similar thing. For those of you who read and understand Chinese (and those that don't!), you may recognise the letter from Master Ku Sanku as from Master Gichin Funakoshi's book 'Ryukyu Tempo Toudi'. Although it was never named in this publication, I thought I would mention it as my own personal homage to this important document.

Bob Sykes and Bernard Taylor of the Colne Valley Black Belt Academy should be thanked here also for providing me with the Karate skills that are used in this novel. Every technique can be performed by myself and every action and reaction has been tested to make sure they are realistic as possible.

I wish to thank my parents for doing the right thing and bringing me up properly. I am a parent myself and only now do I understand everything they went through. I stand in awe of them.

And finally, to everyone who reads this, I hope you enjoyed the story,

Neil

Chapter One

As The Imperial Japanese Army, headed by the leaders of the Satsuma clan and armed with their finest samurai, descended upon the Okinawa capital of Shuri, a gloom had overcome the occupants of the city as if they knew that there would be hard times and repression ahead. However to a select few, the beginning of a resistance was already taking place. In the port towns of Naha and Tomari, there were people developing ways of defending themselves. They were using their own hands and in some areas, their farming tools, which were proving more than capable to defend themselves against the prefecture oppressors. Of course, the Japanese would suppress the Okinawa people and this drove the practice into private. Yet certain people would always stay one step ahead of such things.

One of these people was Chojiro Sakugawa. A follower of the original teachings of the founder of Zen Buddhism, Bodhadiharma or Daruma, he had a meeting to keep with one of his fellow followers about how they were going to get their particular secret off the island and to a safe place. During these dangerous times, it had been deemed illegal to carry a weapon of any kind. For Sakugawa san, this was not something that worried him in particular. On the underground scene there had been rumours of a militant offshoot of people who wanted to take their study to the next level. People were saying that they were studying the principles of Zen Buddhism and where using not just their bodies but their minds as well. Very little was known and it lead to many rumours of this type going around the towns and villages of Okinawa. Sakugawa san smiled to himself while looking around the area he was in. *'If only they knew'*, he thought as he stepped into the street. He carefully looked around and found it was populated by only a few people and they were huddled in groups protecting themselves from the rain. He turned away from them and headed up to his meeting place. When he got there, he waited. Just when his patience was starting to wear a little thin, a figure approached. He wasn't tall, but had a confident gait that suggested he was in charge of this meeting and anything else around him. Nothing was said between the two people until they went inside the little house that was next to the meeting place. When Sakugawa san sat down, he removed his hood to reveal a shaved head. Two deep set brown eyes peered at the still hooded man opposite him before opening his mouth to speak. There was a gap between his two front teeth and a small beard was growing around it, "I have come here to speak about our plans."

The other man returned, "I know. Things are in motion to return it to the heartland over the sea, where our teacher came from."

"How can we do that? The prefecture has a stranglehold on this island and then there are the Chinese as well!"

"This is why the plans must be carefully drawn."

"If people other then our brothers in China get hold of our secret, there could be disaster on a scale we have never known!"

The hooded man paused and then said, "These are dangerous times and we have to do what is needed to return what we have to its rightful place. But with great dangers come great rewards."

Chojiro Sakugawa took a deep breath then said, "The plan cannot be postponed?"

"No."

"Then I will prepare."

"Before you go, Please make sure you see your wife."

"Why?"

The hooded man smiled and said, "She has some news for you. Also, I have something you need for your journey."

With that, the hooded man held out what looked like a small present box, "You will need this when you get to your destination. It holds the key you will need to prove that you have brought it from here."

Sakugawa san looked confused, "Why would I need to do that?"

"You will see."

The conversation was almost over. The hooded man stood up and as he began to walk away he said, "You are going on a journey that is the most important anyone from our brotherhood can do. The box I have given you will give you many friends who will help you to reach your destination. However, you will also have many enemies who will want to stop you. The box is the key to it all. Guard it with your life. Be prepared to die for it. Trust it only to those who your heart trusts. But make sure that the secret it opens lives on. The details of the plan will be given to you soon. Good luck." With that the hooded man left the room.

Chojiro Sakugawa looked at the empty space where he had been. The only thing he could think of was what news could his wife possibly have for him?

Chapter two

Leon Rhodes was settling down to a corona and lime in his living room after a busy day at work which was running the Helme Valley Karate Academy. It was the foremost karate academy in the north of England. Of course Leon, being a cricket and football mad participant, had encouraged his students to use the training methods of other sports and had found that the great loves of his life had provided him with a way to earn a living. Despite this he had another love. Something he kept to himself from his regulars. He was a historian. To be precise, he was a historian of martial arts and had only just begun to put into words the things he had found. He had taken to writing a book surprisingly well, despite being somebody who could not write things down.

Everybody knew him and his wife at the academy and they were well respected for it. They were a team. Wherever one was, the other was close behind and everybody liked them for it. On an average day, you could find the pair of them in the dojo, training hard yet smiling all the way through. Tonight however, Leon was doing nothing except chilling out after a busy Monday night and watching some late night kickboxing on T.V.

Leon was about five foot nine, of medium build with dark brown hair. He had a muscle tone that suggested he did regular physical exercise but had a slight beer gut that also led you to believe he liked a good time. This was the truth. After living like a monk for several years, Leon had decided that he was going to relax a little and enjoy the fruits of his labour. If this meant having the odd beer and lime after work then so be it.

Leon had just finished his first beer and was heading for the fridge to get another when his mobile started to ring. The voice on the other end was familiar.

"You alright lad?"

The caller was Leon's instructor, "I'm getting a team together for a competition and I wondered if you might be interested?"

Leon replied, "When is it?"

"Next week. I was hoping you might enter the Kata competition."

"What? You don't want me to fight?"

"No. You're such a wimp! You couldn't fight your way out of a wet paper bag, even if you tried!"

Leon smiled, "As you asked me so nicely, I think I will enter. Thank you."

"Excellent," said the instructor, "there is one other thing though."

Leon remained silent.

"The competition is part of a weekend extravaganza that involves workshops and seminars and I was hoping you could give a talk on your research into the history of martial arts at the end of competition dinner."

"I knew there would be a reason why you wanted me there," said Leon, completely unsurprised.

"All you have to do is just give a little background of what you are doing," said the instructor in a way that a child explains how easy it is to add two and two to make four..

"I'm not sure it's ready yet," Leon replied.

"Fail to prepare, prepare to fail," said Leon's instructor.

"I can't get out of it then?"

"No, you can't. I've already said you will do it."

"I'd better get prepared then."

"Before you do, I'd speak to your wife first."

Before Leon was about to hang up his phone, His instructor continued.

"Listen, what you are going to do on this evening is really going to cause a stir. What you have researched and found and what you propose is going against the popular grain of thought about our martial arts and how it was taught in the early years. You will have some detractors about your theories but you will also have some people who will agree with you. The main thing you must remember is to trust your heart and say the thing that you truly believe in, OK? I'll see you tomorrow at training. Bye."

With that the instructor disconnected his phone. Leon was stood in his kitchen looking at his unopened bottle of corona wondering what news his wife could possibly have for him.

Chapter three

The grounds of Shuri castle where imposing on the night that Chojiro Sakugawa had been summonsed to learn his fate and place in the grand scheme of his brotherhoods plan. He had long learned this was the seat of power for the Ryukyu kingdom that had been in place before the Satsuma clan instituted the prefecture and he had been someone who could not follow their rule. He considered himself a patriot of Ryukyu and he knew that he was not in a minority. He was someone who had the confidence to believe in the rule of his country, and to do something about it. Others had also not lost the feeling of being part of a sovereign country despite life becoming difficult for all the people of Okinawa since the invasion by the Satsuma clan under the orders of the Japanese emperor. For over a Hundred and seventy years Samurai had been the law of the land. Weapons where banned and if you was found with one on your possession during the many checks upon the inhabitants of the island that took place each year, it would be confiscated after which you would be punished. Punishment usually took the form of a severe beating and because of this many people had taken to learning '*Te*' or 'hands' at the many underground dojos or back gardens of renowned instructors around the island at night.

A voice brought him back to where he was, "I see you are deep in thought."

Sakugawa turned round to come face to face with Yahtsume Takahara, his instructor, "I did not see you Takahara san. I was not *expecting* to see you here."

Takahara smiled and said, "It does not matter what or who you were expecting. The fact that I am here should be enough for you now."

Confused, Sakugawa replied, "Are you here to talk me through the plans?"

"I am here for that purpose. I am also here to give you some advice. But first, please listen to what I have to say. It will not be enough for you just to follow orders blindly without understanding or knowing what it is that you are about to carry, or why you are doing this. What I am about to tell you will give you knowledge that only a select few on this island know."

"I already know a lot of things that people on this island don't know," Sakugawa said, his pride hurt at the thought.

"What I am going to tell you, or more appropriately, show you, will change a lot of things you thought you knew about your studies with me."

"What could be more important than the Daruma's teachings?" asked Sakugawa.

"Nothing could be more important than His teachings. What I am saying is *how* you think we learnt those teachings?" replied Takahara.

"From what you have taught me, it has been passed on from instructor to pupil including Master Ku Sanku who came to this island and formed our brotherhood many years ago."

"Most of that is correct *on this island*," started Takahara, "The clue is Master Ku Sanku. He came to this island with the Daruma's teachings and proceeded to instruct a select few of us what he knew. As our knowledge became stronger and we continued on our paths, Master Ku Sanku became aware of a Satsuma plot to kidnap and kill him. He knew that he would have to leave this island. He also knew it would be dangerous to keep with him alone the secret that is now entrusted to us on this island. So he allowed an even more select few to know the secret that he had to keep to himself all these years."

A wave of comprehension came across Sakugawa's face, "*You* are one of those people?"

"Yes, I am," said Takahara, admiring the look of awe that Sakugawa was now showing him, "That is why you are here. Let us continue."

Chojiro nodded in agreement.

"The teachings Master Ku Sanku gave us are not some random thoughts of an enlightened soul, or his opinion on the teachings that have been passed down over the centuries. If that was to happen then the knowledge would be diluted by other people's opinions and thoughts on how things should be done and the original messages would be lost. The Daruma's teachings would become nothing more than a product of a collection of men. His voice would be lost in a sea of voices. No, Master Ku Sanku taught us the true version of His teachings and we are true practitioners of it."

"But how do you know that this is the case?" Sakugawa asked.

"A question that came to the lips of one of my fellow students during training. It was at the time the Master had discovered this Satsuma plot and he later confided that it was this question that decided his course of action. He looked at us who were his select few and said it was time that we knew the same things he did. With that Master Ku Sanku reached into his robes and pulled out a box. He laid it down in front of us and opened the box to reveal the reason you are now here."

As Takahara talked, he reached into his robes to reveal a box. It was nothing fancy, just plain red. It was about thirty centimetres long, fifteen centimetres wide and about five centimetres deep. If this held a century old secret you would never have known. Sakugawa looked at the box and then Takahara. He was wondering how such an inauspicious thing could hold this amazing secret.

"Is this the same box that you saw?"

"Ah no, that box was so old and battered that since it came into my possession I have replaced it."

"How do I open it?"

"That has already been given to you before you came here to meet me. I trust you have it on you?"

"Yes, I have it with me," replied Sakugawa, thinking of the small present box given to him at his last meeting.

"Well open it then," said Takahara, impatient to get this first part of the game over with.

Sakugawa reached inside his own robes and pulled out the small box. He opened it to reveal a brass key. There were no inscriptions or marks on it. It was just a normal everyday key. He placed it in the hole and twisted. It gave a click and opened slightly. Sakugawa finished opening the lid and looked inside. What he saw was what looked like a book. When he read the one word on the front he reeled in shock and almost fainted. It was as though his world had just been turned upside down. It was the most amazing revelation that anyone in his place could have ever seen.

Chapter four

The assembled throng in the main sports hall of The Helme valley sports centre was buzzing in anticipation at the coming competition of martial arts fighting and kata exhibition from all over the country. This was a prestige event for a lot of the people and the tension was showing in a lot of places. In one corner, competitors from Croyden were running through the moves of the kata that they were going to show. Meanwhile, a fighter from Sheffield was psyching himself up for his first fight by meditating in a corner before standing up and repeatedly slapping himself across the face in an attempt to make him focused enough for the ensuring combat.

Leon looked across at the fighter. He was glad that he wasn't in the fighting competition. After many years of hard knocks from fellow combatants, he was starting to mellow. Of course, his age and experience had something to do with it, but there was also an intuition that he was meant to do other things. An acute mind, which is always a bonus in martial arts, was taking him down a path away from fighting, yet he knew that his days involved in competitions of some sort where far from over. That was why he had entered into the kata demonstration competition instead. These feelings were re-enforced by the conversation he had with his wife, Sarah, five days ago.

"Good morning, how are you?" said Leon that fateful Sunday morning as he handed over some toast and a cup of tea while she was still in bed.

"I'm fine, darling." replied Sarah.

"I had a message from a friend of ours saying I needed to speak to you," began Leon, "so what is it that you need to tell me?"

Sarah looked as if Leon had just hit her with something hard and heavy across her face. She put the piece of toast that was in her hand down on the plate she was holding and began to fidget.

"What? Has something happened?" said Leon looking concerned.

"Well yes, something has happened. I'm not sure how you are going to take it," replied Sarah.

"Look, just put me out of my misery will you?"

"OK. I want you to know that I love you and I know what I am about to tell you is going to change our lives very much, but......I'm pregnant."

"WHAT!!!? How?"

"Well, I thought that might be obvious," said Sarah shyly.

"Yes I know how. But when? Where? Why!?" Leon was blustering, quite obviously in shock.

"You know that day I came back from Spain?" asked Sarah.

A wave of comprehension came across Leon's face. He looked at his wife and said, "How do you know?"

"This," she handed Leon a pregnancy test, which showed a positive result. Leon looked at it in complete awe. He had never considered having a family before now and here it was in full view.

"I'm going to get a newspaper. I'll be back soon."

"Leon!" shouted Sarah, but Leon was already halfway down the stairs. He put his left shoe on his right foot and his right shoe on his left foot, grabbed his dressing gown thinking it was a coat and walked out of his house. He headed straight for the local newsagent, bought a newspaper, two miniature bottles of brandy and a ten pack of cigarettes.

He walked onto an adjoining field to his house, smoked five of the cigarettes, and drunk the two bottles of brandy. On the way back to his house, he threw away the pack of cigarettes. When he got home he went straight to the bathroom, brushed his teeth, and then rinsed with mouthwash before dousing himself with his favourite scent, Lacoste red. He then headed back into his bedroom where he found Sarah still in bed.

She looked up expectantly at him, "Well?"

"Here's your paper love."

"And?"

Leon swept her into his arms and kissed her, "It's wonderful. Shame you were going for black belt!"

Sarah gave Leon a playful slap across the shoulder.

A voice from a PA system brought Leon back from his thoughts, "And now Leon Rhodes will perform the kata Ku Shanku!"

The audience clapped politely while Leon made his way to the centre of the mat. He stood to attention before bowing to the judges in front of him. He took the *yoi* position and began the kata.

Ku Shanku is the longest kata in his style of karate and it took several minutes to perform. When he had finished the final move and provided the accompanying *Kiyai,* he turned, and bowed to the judges again, before walking off to applause from the crowd. Leon wasn't too worried whether he had turned in a competition winning performance but he liked to think that it might be something close. Either way, he thought it didn't matter as he had something bigger going on that put things into perspective.

"That was great Leon!" said his instructor, Kenneth, "If you don't get a placed finish then the judges must be blind!"

"We'll see Ken," replied Leon

"Since when did you become so coy?"

Leon looked at Ken and smiled, "You know why. I'll just go and get changed."

Leon went to the changing rooms and changed out of his white *gi* and showered before putting on his trademark shirt, jeans, tan coloured leather shoes and black jacket. He made his way back into the sports hall just as they were announcing medallists for the competitions, "...and the winner of the freestyle fighting is.....Steve Walsh!" It was the fighter who Leon had seen slapping himself round the face earlier.

"Now for the kata competition. In third place, John Simons!" There was applause as he came to the front of the judges to receive his trophy.

"In second place, Dave Johnson!" more applause as he also came to the front to receive his trophy.

"And the winner of this years Helme Valley kata competition is.....Leon Rhodes!" Leon looked completely taken aback. He made his way to the judges and took his trophy. It was considerably larger then the other two trophies. But what made him look twice was the way the judge handed it to him. There was a look of knowing on the gentleman's face that made Leon think he may have met him before, but he couldn't think where. He made a mental note to ask Kenneth when he had chance. After the obligatory photos and round of applause, everybody started to make their way out of the sports hall. In a couple of hours time Leon would be the guest after dinner speaker at the meal held for all martial artists attending the event. He made his way home to change. Sarah was over the moon at another trophy for the mantelpiece and had cleared a space on it when Leon returned. She was almost ready, while Leon still hadn't got into his dinner suit.

"Come on Leon, we can't be late!"

"I'm having problems with this bow tie."

"Come here," she made towards him and expertly did his tie for him.

"Thanks Sarah."

"Hurry up; the taxi will be arriving in fifteen minutes."

"You know, I've got a funny feeling about tonight."

"Look, you're just nervous. Everything will be fine," soothed Sarah.

Leon quickly finished getting into his suit and a short while later they were in the taxi heading for Helme Hall Hotel where the dinner would take place. Ten minutes later they were walking through the entrance and into the drinks reception where Sarah took the offered orange juice while Leon had a glass of champagne thrust into his hand.

They hadn't even had time to settle when the bell had rung for dinner to be served. Kenneth as president of the welcoming karate club collared Leon and Sarah just as they were about to walk into the function suite.

"Hold on you two, I have to announce you to the rest of the guests!"

They waited just by the entrance while Kenneth walked in and took his seat. They heard a knocking of wood on wood and Kenneth's booming voice, "Ladies and Gentlemen please welcome our guests of honour tonight, Leon and Sarah Rhodes!" Everybody stood up and started to clap as Leon and Sarah entered the room. They took their seats at the top table and very quickly the hotel staff started to serve the food.

After all the courses had been served (Leon particularly enjoyed his dessert of tiramisu!), and the conversations had run dry, Kenneth stood and knocked on the table for everybody's attention. The room became silent, "It gives me great pleasure to introduce a real thinker amongst the martial arts community here in West Yorkshire. He has researched and personally shown me the history and culture of the very things which unite us all here tonight. He has a unique insight into the ways our predecessors taught our art and has some very thought provoking arguments I think will change the way we think about our arts. Plus he's also bloody good at Ku Shanku!" There was laughter around the room, "So please Ladies and Gentlemen, allow me to introduce Leon Rhodes!"

Applause rung around the function suite as Leon stood up and Kenneth sat down, "Thank you Ken for your kind words to introduce me. Let me just say that the two hundred quid I gave to all the judges was a worthwhile investment!" again the room rang with laughter. "OK, where do I begin? I have been asked to talk you today about my research and to share with you some of my findings, so I am going to introduce to you all the most interesting part of it. As we all know the modern day karate that we study originated from Okinawa. The instructors of old passed down their teaching to pupil after pupil. But where did these teachings come from? Some people say that Karate is a combination of opinions and interpretations which change from generation to generation and is different from area to area, with certain great instructors in history having some long term influence on each branch of martial art. I am not so sure this is the case, entirely. What if I was to tell you that these ancient instructors had an even more ancient manual with which to work from? A manual which gave them a framework to give instruction to their students and something which was written by the originator of all martial arts. The person I am referring to is, of course, Bodhadiharma or Daruma. The book I am referring to is the...

Chapter five

"Bubishi!" cried Sakugawa.

"Yes," exclaimed Takahara, "this is the secret we have kept all these years and what is now in danger."

"But this was only rumoured to exist," continued Chojiro, "a text that you have based all your teachings on is surely dangerous to have. If it fell into the wrong hands, the reason we are here is surely going to come under threat. Everything we have built up and taught would disappear. The enemy would simply destroy it and over time we would slowly disappear as the teachings and practices would be forgotten!"

"Another reason is should it fall into the wrong hands, the secrets we have learnt will become known to our enemy. They will have the same knowledge as us and our advantage would be lost. That is the reason you are here Chojiro," Takahara said. The use of his first name was what caught Sakugawa's attention. His instructor had never used it before, until now. "You are the youngest and most gifted student our brotherhood has ever taught. The rest of us are getting old. We, as elders in the brotherhood, are not up to a journey that involves hundreds of miles and countless threats and dangers. That is why we are letting you see our secret and why we are commanding you to go on this journey."

Chojiro was still reeling from the shock of what he had just discovered, "I am to do this journey alone?"

"No, you may take with you anybody who you feel might prove useful to you during your journey."

"How do I get across the sea?" Sakugawa asked.

"Safe passage has been booked for you at the port of Naha. You will leave in two days time," replied Takahara.

"When I get to the mainland, how will I know where to go?"

"You will meet up with a representative of our brotherhood in China. This person will tell you how to proceed. All I can tell you is that you are to make your way to the Daruma's temple in Henan province. The details of how you will get there will be revealed when you meet your contact."

"I know of people who can help me," said Sakugawa.

"Good," started Takahara, "I suggest you speak to them. You have everything you need. I hope you succeed. For everyone's sake."

"I will not fail you."

As Sakugawa turned to leave the meeting there was a rustle from behind him. He turned back towards his instructor to see that there were people coming towards him and Takahara. As they moved closer,

Sakugawa could see that they were the samurai of the Satsuma clan and their intentions looked far from peaceful.

"Why are you here?" exclaimed the leader of the group of ten samurai.

"We are friends taking a walk, smelling the fresh air and enjoying such a scenic area together," replied Takahara.

"We have reason to believe that enemies of the Prefecture are meeting here to conspire against us. We see no one here but you. Explain yourselves!" exclaimed the leader.

"As I said....," began Takahara but as he said it, a member of the samurai attacked him with a swipe of his sword that started from below his belt and intended to take his head clean off. Takahara simply and calmly took a step back and the attack missed by mere inches. Despite this, he looked meekly at the leader of the group and said, "You are attacking myself and my friend for merely being here when you have no proof of what we are doing other than what you have been told or what you think we are doing?" said Takahara matter-of-factly.

"Sensei, please, lets just go. I wish for no confrontation," said Sakugawa.

"Nor do I, Chojiro," replied Takahara.

"You are in an area that has been identified as holding an illegal meeting. We intend to find out what you are doing!" the leader of the samurai said.

"I see I have no choice. Chojiro please go," Takahara said to his pupil.

"No sensei! My place is beside you," replied Sakugawa.

"Very well."

As Takahara said his last sentence another samurai took this as his cue and attacked him. Takahara stepped to one side and with a heavy handed blow to the back of the head knocked his assailant clean out. Another samurai went for Sakugawa. He decided that caution was the better part of valour and stepped into the encounter carefully. He swiped for Sakugawa's mid rift which Chojiro moved away from with ease. Again he went for the mid rift and Sakugawa repeated his move. The distance between the two of them was increasing and Sakugawa noticed this. The samurai lunged a little further hoping to catch him off guard but he had stretched a little more than was needed and Sakugawa took this as his cue. He jumped up turned his body round and caught his attacker with a spinning hook kick that knocked the samurai out. Two down, eight to go.

The leader saw the turn of events and realised that one on one, his warriors were not going to defeat his enemy, so he sent another four of them into battle, two on each of his enemy, despite this Takahara and Sakugawa were defending themselves to the hilt. The turning point of the battle came when the leader correctly identified that Takahara would come to the defence of his friend whom the rest of his team he sent against.

"Go, Chojiro. Please go!" as he fended off an attack from several samurai.

"I can't sensei! I should be by your side!" replied Sakugawa.

"You must," as he swiped away at an arm holding a sword from his enemy, "your safety is the most important thing now!"

Chojiro was about to enter the battle that Takahara had endured when the decision to run was made for him. A samurai had seen that Takahara had turned away from him, or towards Sakugawa, and wasn't paying attention to the defence of his right shoulder. He let rip with his sword and speared it. Takahara let out an almighty scream. With a little difficulty, he removed the sword from his shoulder and turned it upon his attacker with a breathtaking agility that removed the samurai's hands from his wrists. The samurai crumpled in agony cradling his bleeding stumps. As he was about to turn upon another attacker, the leader of the samurai had moved in and took a swipe at Takahara's left shoulder. It connected and removed the arm from the elbow and he dropped to his knees. Sakugawa had now started to slide away as the samurai moved in for the kill. Takahara still had a sword in his right hand and with another arc of the sword, which took all his apparent strength and might, he slit the throat of the leader who fell to the floor with an almighty thump. There was just the three attackers left now and they were moving toward Takahara with an unmistakable menace who realising that his time was now short exclaimed, "You will not win, Satsuma clan! The secret lives on!"

With that Takahara lifted off his haunches and attacked the three remaining samurai. With a guttural shout he took the head clean off one his attackers as he ran past them. Sakugawa was watching on in awe at the most amazing person he had ever seen fighting. He watched Takahara turn at his two remaining enemies and rush at them once again. This time it was not to be. As Takahara ran at them he looked at Sakugawa. *Now!* Chojiro took that as his cue. He ran as fast as he could away from the scene of this fight. The samurai did not follow. He quickly took a turn round to look at the scene that he was leaving and wished that he had not done so. Takahara was impaled upon a sword through his heart. He had a look of complete surprise in his eyes. As Sakugawa watched he saw the other samurai move in and with one clean swoop, he decapitated Takahara where he knelt. Chojiro's last ever view of his sensei was of a sword been removed from his torso and his body fall to the floor completely devoid of the life and spirit which ran through him.

As he left the grounds of Shuri castle, he looked at the two boxes now in his possession with tears in his eyes and wondered exactly what he had let himself in for. After everything that had gone on tonight, he made the decision to see the three other people he knew in his heart he could trust. The problem was, one of them was his wife.

Chapter six

"…..Bubishi." said Leon.

A silence was met with his last word. There were rumours among the local martial arts community that this was what he was researching. Nobody knew what he had found, or what theories he was proposing. Many people had heard of the existence of this book, but knew very little about it. Leon meanwhile looked at the room who were listening attentively. Although his research found information relatively easy, what he wanted to do with that information was speculate at the possible origins of the book. This was what Ken had found so interesting and thought provoking. Many of the original theories they came up with were dismissed as pure nonsense by the pair of them during their many late night bottles of wine and discussion marathons. After many months of research, discussion and argument, they were beginning to form a few theories which seemed possible. He looked at Ken who was smiling as though he was enjoying the same thoughts as Leon.

"The existence of this book is well known. I'm sure you have all heard of it. But for those who haven't, I'll give a brief synopsis. The Bubishi is an early descriptive text for the founding martial artists which first came to light in the early twentieth century. It was published in part and without translation by Funakoshi, the founder of Shotokan karate, in 1930. It wasn't until 1942 that the full version was discovered. It has been used and revered by several great masters including the founder of Goju-ryu karate, Chojun Miyagi. It is a set of pictures, notes and recipes for being an accomplished martial artist, Zen Buddhist and Chinese medicine practitioner. In fact, this is a book for the person who wishes to conduct themselves according to the White Crane or Shaolin Fist Kung fu teachings. Its origins are unknown and shrouded in mystery. What I am writing at the moment, is an investigation into its origins. Information on this subject is sketchy at best and because of this, what I am writing is mostly speculation. So, what is it that I am speculating? At the moment, I have come up with three theories so far....."

Leon went into the first one, which was about the Bubishi being a notebook of a student from early China, which got copied down many times throughout history. Leon noted that he thought this was the most likely.

The second theory was that it doesn't have as much history as first thought. The people who published it were the originators of the book or, as part two to the theory; it is a document from Okinawa written by somebody documenting their studies during the occupation by the Japanese. Leon said this was the next most likely theory.

The last theory was that this was a truly historical document of sizeable proportions. This is in fact the teachings or at the very least a first hand written record of the personal teachings of the Daruma himself making it the martial arts equivalent of The Bible, or The Koran. "It goes without saying that I think this is the most unlikely of the theories," said Leon, smiling almost apologetically. There was appreciative and understanding smiling and nodding from the audience, except one person. Leon noticed him immediately as the man who handed him his trophy at the competition. He was watching Leon with a mixture of interest and concern as though he was listening to something he didn't like.

"This is what I'm researching. The wheels are in motion and I will have a few more theories by the time the book is published. What I have done tonight is share with you a little of what I am writing. If you find it interesting, then please buy the book when it is published. Thank you for taking the time to listen." Leon sat down. The audience stood and applauded. Apart from one person, again. As Leon took the applause, he turned to his left and saw the gentleman still sat down, looking straight at him. The man smiled slightly and raised his glass before draining its contents. He never once took his eyes off him. Unsettled, Leon continued to take the applause.

Once it had died down, people started to come to the top table, say thank you to Ken and Leon before making their way out of the function suite.

"Come on lad, I'll buy you a beer before we go home," said Ken as he made his way out of the suite to the bar. He bought a bottle of corona and lime, an orange juice and a pint of best bitter and directed them to a table by the big bay windows which are a feature of these Georgian mansion hotels.

"Ken, can I ask a question?" said Leon as he sat down.

"Sure, fire away," replied Ken

"What's the name of the guy who gave me my trophy today?"

Ken eyed him suspiciously, "Why do you want to know?"

"Just answer my question," Leon said with a touch of impatience.

"His name is Malcolm Gaines. He is the benefactor of the event we hosted this weekend. He is the president of a sports equipment manufacturer which just so happens to make the belts, gi and protective equipment for sports martial arts that we use at the academy and in competitions like this one. He is also an enthusiastic patron of all martial arts. He collects rare and unique items from history and puts them on display at his factory. I'm like a kid in a sweetshop whenever I visit that place. I'll take you there one day."

"Thanks. Why did he not like what I was saying after dinner then?"

"He probably just disagrees with you, Leon. Don't worry about it."

"I'm not sure. He didn't like what I was saying, but I don't think it was because he disagreed though."

"Look, Malcolm Gaines lives and breathes Martial arts. Not only does he practice Shotokan and Wado-Ryu karate, he is currently studying Pencak Silat and Defendo. He is also an historian of the arts. He is probably doing the same research as you too. He disagrees with you because he has come to different conclusions or has some sort of professional rivalry. I said that this would happen. You were always going to divide people with this subject. However, you started your speech correctly and pointed out that it was theory which you were proposing with a little backing of research and your opinion. Most people understood and were quite happy to listen. But you are going to get the odd *snob* who says that you are a young pretender who thinks he knows it all. Despite all the good things Malcolm does for our arts, he is the biggest snob of them all. Don't lose any sleep over it, OK?"

"Sorry Ken, I still wasn't prepared for people's negative reactions. I thought they would all be positive."

"And they were. Out of two hundred people, you had one negative reaction. If I was you, I would take that. In fact, that was better than I thought you was going to get. I thought at least ten people would walk out tonight. One of them I expected to be Malcolm and even he stayed to listen to it all. You just have to remember this is a controversial subject."

Leon smiled back at Ken. Despite the fact that he was nearly twice Leon's age, he considered Ken a friend and not a father figure. Ken pushed him to extremes as Leon's instructor during training but after it, the friendship resumed and Leon considered Ken's opinion to be the most important to him, after Sarah's of course. It was because of this that Leon decided perhaps Ken was right and he shouldn't give it too much thought.

They continued their discussions on the weekend's events before finishing their drinks and going their separate ways. Leon and Sarah caught a taxi home, while Ken walked the hundred yards to his house. When they arrived, there was an envelope waiting on the doormat as they walked through the front door. Leon put it on the mantelpiece before putting Sarah to bed. He went back downstairs and opened it. There was a piece of paper inside. Leon unfolded it and read the message which was written,

'We need to speak. I would appreciate it if you came to my place on the 30th June at 7PM. My address is 27 Ascot Drive. Malcolm Gaines.'

Leon looked at the letter in bewilderment. Malcolm Gaines had personally got in touch and was asking to speak to him. The 30th was two days away and the answer would present itself then. There was no point him worrying about it. With that, Leon helped himself to a corona and lime and sat in front of the TV until he had finished his drink. He made his way upstairs and went to bed at just after one O'clock in the morning.

The next thing he knew, he was woken up by a loud thud on the door. Leon looked at the alarm clock beside his bed which read 6.30 in the morning. He got up wondering who on earth would be knocking on his door at this time. As he opened it, his jaw dropped as he was greeted by the sight of two police riot vans, two police cars, at least 20 police officers, of which half of them were armed and two plain clothed detectives in front of him. The nearest plain clothed police officer was showing him his badge while saying, "Leon Rhodes? I'm arresting you on suspicion of murder...."

Chapter seven

Sakugawa got home twenty minutes after leaving Shuri castle. He walked in to find his wife, Shumi, waiting anxiously for his return, "Chojiro! Where have you been? I've been so worried. I have not seen you in nearly twelve hours."

"I'm sorry, I've been busy. I should have stopped off to see you on my way to meet Takahara san."

"It's OK. You're here now," she smiled. "Have you eaten? Would you like me to prepare you something?"

Chojiro's heart was heavy with sadness after what had happened. He could not hide this from his wife. "Is everything OK? Has something happened? Have you had an argument with Takahara san again?"

"No Shumi, I have not," Chojiro's legs felt suddenly tired and he had to sit down. As he did so, he put his head in his hands.

"What's the matter then?" asked his wife.

"Something has happened. We were attacked by the samurai while I was talking to him."

"No! You both walked away I hope."

Chojiro looked at his wife. His eyes were beginning to well with tears and his throat was starting to seize up. All he could do was shake his head.

"Where have they taken him? Can't you get everybody together and try to break him out of wherever it is they take prisoners?"

"The samurai do not take prisoners, Shumi," said Chojiro. This statement brought a tense respite to the conversation. The longer the pause went on, the plainer it became to Shumi that her husband's mentor was perhaps no longer with them.

"You mean-"

"Yes, Shumi, He died defending me and his secret," as he pulled the two boxes out of his robes. Shumi took a look at them

"He died defending two boxes? What is so important in those boxes that the Satsuma wants?"

"If I tell you, I would be breaking an oath I made to him before he died," replied Chojiro as he replaced them in his robes.

"What are you going to do now?" asked Shumi.

"I'm returning to the Dojo. I need guidance. The Elders will be able to provide it."

"Then I am coming too," Shumi said, with a dangerous glint in her eye. There was no way Chojiro was going to argue with her.

"Very well. I suggest you get some belongings together."

"We are not returning here?"

"It is a possibility, Shumi," said Chojiro.

With that, she rushed from the room and began to pack a few belongings.

"Do not take too much; we may be going on a long journey. You need to keep things as light as possible," he called to her.

"Where are we going?" asked Shumi.

"I can't tell you yet. When we begin then I will say."

Shumi came back into the room with a small sack. In it was a few clothes and some treasured belongings for both of them. Without a word they left their small house and began making their way to the Dojo.

* * * * * * * * * * * *

The pair arrived at the Dojo ten minutes later. As they were making their way to the entrance, there was a quietness which did not seem right. Normally there were people walking around and others practicing moves, shapes and form. Chojiro's senses became suddenly alert. Something was wrong, very wrong.

"Wait here," he signalled to his wife.

If she was going to argue, Chojiro couldn't say as he began to make his way through the entrance. All was very quiet and still. Chojiro's hearing intensified in preparation for an attack, but it never came. As he walked into the dojo, he was greeted with a sight of carnage and destruction that he had never seen before. All around the room, the bodies of the elders and his fellow students lay where they had been slain. As far as he could see, he was the only one left until he heard a rustle in a room which led off to his left.

He silently made his way towards the room. He could see movement in there. He ran into the room and was about to attack whoever was there, when a familiar voice shouted, "Stop Chojiro! It's me!"

Kosaku Funakoshi cowered into a corner expecting Chojiro to attack at any moment. At the sight of such a treasured friend, Chojiro stopped himself. The fact that one of the people he trusted was in front of him now, made him stop what he was doing. He walked over to his friend and offered his hand, "Kosaku, I feared the worst. I'm sorry if I gave you the impression you were my enemy. I can clearly see you are not. What happened here?"

"Chojiro, I'm so glad to see you. The Satsuma came here and did this. They were asking about boxes and keys. No one knew what they were talking about. We couldn't give them an answer. When the samurai heard this, they ran riot. All I could do was go into hiding. I'm sorry, I know I should have joined our brothers in defending the dojo..." his voice trailed off.

"Don't be ashamed Kosaku; what you have done is far more than you will ever know. The fact that you are alive is reason to believe that the journey set before me is evermore necessary. I wish you to join me on it. Will you come?"

"What do I have to stay for, Chojiro," as he intimated around him.

"First Kosaku, we must make this area pure and clean," replied Chojiro, "I'm sorry to involve you in this task, but it is something we must do. The slain here must be laid to rest."

Shumi came into the dojo holding a pair of spades, "I found these by the herb garden. I thought they might be needed."

"Thank you, Shumi, "said Chojiro, gratefully, "let us begin."

With that, Chojiro walked outside and found a suitable clearing near the dojo, put his foot on the edge of the spade and began to dig the graves.

After many hours hard work, the three of them had finished the job. Chojiro had one last job to do. He walked over to the nearest tree and broke off a branch. He tore off the sleeves to his robes and wrapped them around the branch while walking to the fire that Shumi had set a few hours earlier to keep her warm while the two men dug. He touched it to the crackling flames before walking over to the dojo. With sadness in his eyes, he set fire to the place where he had known so much happiness and contentment over his short number of years. As he watched the it engulf in flames, resolve started to form in his eyes and his spirit at the upcoming journey he knew he would have to undertake. The group he wanted to take with him needed one more member. "Come, Shumi, Kosaku. We need to go."

"Where are we going, Chojiro?" replied Funakoshi.

"To see another good friend, Kosaku"

With that, they left the dojo for the last time. As they walked away, groups of people began to converge on the building, wondering what was happening. Panicked voices trailed away as people rushed to organize the putting out of the flames. Chojiro could hear the samurai barking orders. *'At least they are occupied. They will be too busy to look for me,'* he thought.

Sakugawa led the way, while Shumi and Kosaku followed. He led them back into the town before taking a left after a short distance. The place they were going was somewhere that Chojiro had been to only a few hours ago. He knew that this person would be watching the area after everything that had happened and would come to the little house when he saw Chojiro there. He had received the first of the two boxes here and knew that the person who had given it to him would want to help. When he arrived at the house, he sat down and began to meditate. Kosaku and Shumi looked on, unsure what they were meant to do. After a while, they found places to sit down and began to patiently wait for whoever it was that Chojiro was waiting for. After a few hours had passed, two men approached. One of whom had a confident gait that suggested he was in charge of the situation. The other man was also somebody Chojiro knew very well. The fact that they were together surprised him, but Chojiro was not going to show this.

"I see you have returned, Chojiro, "said the confident man.

"I am in need of your assistance," he replied.

"What is it you ask of me?"

"I have been asked to take a journey that will take me many months, miles and time to achieve. I need your presence, guidance, wisdom and strength to help me achieve it. Will you join me?" asked Chojiro.

The confident man took a moment to reflect, "The brotherhood has sent you here. I take it they are in trouble?"

"We are all that is left," replied Chojiro.

Without hesitation the confident man replied, "I, Jano Miyagi, am at your service."

Chojiro looked at Jano, before turning to the man on his right, "I did not come here looking for a fifth person to join us on our journey, Gogen Mabuni. However you are here and I cannot and will not exclude you from this."

Gogen Mabuni looked at Chojiro and said, "When the samurai attacked your dojo, I knew my calling. Chojiro Sakugawa, I wish to help you on your journey."

Chojiro stood and looked at the assembled group and saw that they were the last assembled people of the brotherhood he had been a member of since he was a child. He knew that his destiny lay in the hands of the people assembled around him, "It's time we left this place and head to the port of Naha. Our passage away from this island waits."

As they left their home town, Chojiro thought that it had been too easy to recruit the members of the party. He would endeavour to find out why. As he left it, he looked back at Shuri and wondered if he would ever see it again.

CHAPTER EIGHT

As Leon looked round his cell, he wondered, *'how on earth have I managed to end up here?'*

He had been a guest speaker at a function and enjoyed a drink with his friend afterwards, before going home with his wife and went to bed. When he woke up he was arrested and was now here, in a cell at the police station in Huddersfield. A loud clunk from someone turning the lock on the door of his cell brought Leon from his thoughts.

"The detective wishes to begin your interview now, sir," said the holding sergeant, "this way if you please."

Leon followed the police officer thinking it was very strange that despite being held for murder he was being addressed as sir. He continued to follow the officer while being flanked by two more until they reached the interview room. He followed them in before sitting down on one of the chairs. The policemen left the room and Leon was left on his own to look at his own reflection in the mirror. *'Someone behind it, no doubt'.* He noticed that he looked tired. The bags under his eyes were as big as saucers. It only served to remind Leon that he could do with a cup of tea right now.

After about five minutes of waiting, the detective who was to interview Leon walked in. He was about six foot one, Afro-Caribbean with a shaved head and a goatee beard. He had an imposing air about him as though he was not going to mess about with the subject and get straight to the point. He sat down while always keeping an eye on Leon as though he might make a run at any moment. Not that he needed to as Leon had no intention to do so.

The detective took out a cassette tape from a file he had carried into the room and placed it into the machine, pressed the record button and waited a few seconds. As he did so, a woman also walked into the room and sat down beside the man. She was in her late twenties, had blonde hair and carried a little excess weight. She had glasses that were quite thick rimmed and her shoulder length hair was tucked behind her ears.

"The date is Friday, 29th of June. The time is ten thirty-seven AM. Present in the room is Detective superintendent Victor Ugiagbe, Detective Sergeant Susan Jones and...." The man gesticulated towards Leon who leaned and forward and said, "Leon Rhodes."

"We are here to conduct an interview regarding the murder of Malcolm Gaines on the night of 28th of June..."

"What? Malcolm Gaines is dead!" exclaimed Leon.

"Yes, he was beheaded."

None of this was making any sense to Leon. He knew he had nothing to do with this. Plus, he had no weapon in his possession that would be able to behead a person.

Victor looked at Leon and tried to size him up. He thought he was dealing with one very cool customer. The expression of innocence at the news was convincing yet Leon had not seen the full extent of the evidence. Once he did, the truth would start to show itself. Of that, Victor was certain.

Susan looked at the pair of them and thought that this was going to be an interesting game today. Who was telling the truth? She had seen the evidence and it did make a case against the suspect. However, the real reason that they were all here was the need to get information into the background behind this case. Victor being his usual self had decided to make Leon a suspect to be able to bring him in. Susan's job was to get through to the interviewee and get an insight into what had happened. If they got a confession at the same time then it was a double result. However, Leon's reaction to the news that someone he knew was dead was very good acting, or a genuine reaction to something he had not previously heard. Either way, Susan decided to sit on the fence and see this game played out.

"Tell me, what sort of weapon can you imagine would be able to do that sort of damage to the human body?" asked Victor.

Leon sensed a leading question, but answered it nonetheless, "I don't know, there are many things. A chainsaw, knife, axe, sword…"

Victor butted in, "Yes, sword seems an appropriate one here. What swords are you aware of in your profession?"

'There are many, you twat!' thought Leon.

"The Scottish claymore, the rapier, the foil and the scimitar. There are quite a few. You'll have to be a little more specific here. There are many similarities in the uses of a weapon. For example, eskrimadors and fencers use different weapons but there are many similarities in their stances and weapon holding. Yet one is French and English influenced and one is Malaysian. They are two separate cultures, but they have developed similar theories."

'Playing it cool here is this one,' thought Victor.

"I was thinking of something a little bit more up your street. A little more oriental."

As far as Leon was concerned there was only one thing that meant, "Samurai…."

"Yes, samurai Mr Rhodes. I'd like to put onto the record that I am showing Mr Rhodes exhibit four one two A." as Victor showed Leon a picture he had removed from the file by his right hand, "As you can see, this shows a pair of samurai swords which have blood on them. The blood has been identified as Mr Gaines."

"Where was the swords found?"

"They were found on their mounts in Mr Gaines Museum."

"The museum at his factory?

'*Strike one*' thought Victor, '*You've never seen his museum. How do you know that those swords belong there?*'

"How can you be sure that Malcolm Gaines has been murdered?" asked Leon as he looked at the photograph.

"This. I am know showing Mr Rhodes exhibit four one two G," as Victor removed another picture from the file. Leon looked at it and was very nearly sick. Malcolm Gaines head was shown completely removed from its body. Leon could tell this as the body it should have been attached to was no where in sight. Malcolm's eyes had rolled into his head and his mouth was open in a slightly surprised fashion. Leon gave the picture back as Victor said, "His head was found about five metres from his body. It was a particularly gruesome scene."

"At the moment all I see is a murdered man. I want to know why I am here," said Leon, as he tried to recover from the sight he had just seen.

"Malcolm kept a diary, if you didn't know. In it are constant references to you. His entries show that you were following research that he was conducting himself and that you were plagiarising everything he had found. The entries show that he thought it was only a matter of time before the two of you met. In fact, we know that there was going to be a meeting between the two of you and he was so scared of your presence he was planning on having protection with him when that happened. We know that meeting was due to be tomorrow."

'*Yes it was*' thought Leon, '*but I never knew he was scared of me,*'

"Mr Rhodes, I'm going to show you some excerpts from his diary. For the record, I'm showing Mr Rhodes exhibit four one two C."

Leon took the evidence. It was a book that was torn and tattered with extra sheets added to it. He opened it at a place that was bookmarked and started to read at a particular entry dated the 3rd of March:-

'*Bubishi is evermore further from the Yakuza. Yet Leon Rhodes tries to get closer with every step. He must be made to see what he is looking at is something I know and protect everyday. He is a hardy soul worthy of the knowledge, but he must realise that with every step he takes, he comes closer to the knowledge he must not yet know. I fear that as every day passes, he will bring into the open knowledge that I have worked so hard to keep secret. I must speak to him but I find it difficult to contact him. He must not know how close he is to finding my secret.'*

"Were you blackmailing him, Mr Rhodes?" asked Victor when Leo had finished reading.

"Are you mad? Of course I wasn't!" replied Leon.

As she watched this interview unfold, a thought occurred to Susan Jones, *'this bloke is innocent.'*

"According to the evidence, I would say that you knew something about him that he did not want bringing out in the open." said Victor.

"I never met the man until this afternoon," exclaimed Leon

Susan decided that this was her time, "Could I have a word, please Victor?"

Victor looked at her before saying, "Sure Susan. Interview suspended at ten fifty five."

Susan made to leave the room and Victor followed.

"What do you want to talk to me about?" asked Victor as he closed the door behind him.

"I'm not so sure that you have the right man here," replied Susan.

"What makes you think that?"

"He's quite clearly in shock at the news you have given him. What you have is purely circumstantial at the moment. We don't even have evidence that he has been to his house yet."

"He is involved in this. I want to find out why."

"Then let's find out why," replied Susan, "just lay off him a bit. The truth will come out. We don't need to lay on to him so hard."

Victor thought for a second. It was usually Susan's way to intervene like this and to be honest she had not yet proved him wrong. There was something to be said for a woman's intuition.

"OK. It's your call," said Victor, "the minute we have something close to a confession though, I'm taking over."

"There won't be a confession, we just need information."

With that, the pair of them returned to the interview room and Victor depressed the pause button on the tape recorder, "Interview recommenced at ten fifty seven."

Susan took over, "Mr Rhodes, it is quite clear from our evidence that you were in some sort of competition with the deceased. Can you think why?"

"The only thing I can think of is that I am researching some history of martial arts," replied Leon, "I know he was a big contributor to our arts and was a historian like myself."

"What were you researching, Mr Rhodes?" asked Susan.

"I was looking at an ancient text which is reputed to be the precursor of martial arts."

"Did you have reason to believe he was some sort rival?"

"Until yesterday, no I did not." As the words left Leon's mouth he realised he had said the wrong thing.

Strike two, thought Victor. Here was an admission of motive.

Leon continued, "I didn't even know he was looking into the same thing. The only reason I knew was because my instructor told me so after my speech."

He has cover stories. This might prove more difficult.

"Your speech?"

"Yes, I gave a speech at the after competition dinner at The Helme Hall Hotel. I was having a drink with Kenneth, my instructor. He told me that Malcolm was researching the same thing," said Leon.

Susan looked at Victor. She knew that this was not going according to his plan. He expected this to be cut and dried but things were not going right at all. Leon Rhodes wouldn't crack. Not because he was an expert at proving himself innocent but because she felt he *was* proving himself innocent.

"Where did you go after speaking to your instructor?" asked Susan.

"I went home," replied Leon, "It was there that I found the note that asked me to meet Malcolm. I have a witness to say that was where I am and I still have the note to prove that Malcolm initiated contact with me."

"We will check."

"You do that," said Leon, "then you can see that this whole thing is completely ridiculous," He had had enough of being polite anymore. He knew this was a complete waste of time. He was innocent.

"There is one more thing, Leon. There are constant references to the Bubishi and his trying to keep it secret. Why would he want to keep this secret from you?" Susan said.

"I don't know. I certainly had no reason to be his enemy."

"Could you give us a moment please, Leon," As Susan stood, "Interview suspended at eleven ten AM."

Susan left the interview room. Victor quickly followed. "There is something going on. However I believe that Leon did not kill Malcolm Gaines. I think it might be a good idea to cut him loose and keep an eye on him," said Susan.

"You think he is involved?" asked Victor.

"Possibly. Not as the murderer, but he knows the person or will lead us to them."

"OK. This is going to hurt but I'll trust your judgement."

"Thanks Vic."

They entered the interview room, as Leon was looking at his reflection again. The mirror told him that someone was watching his every move. Leon didn't like this big brother feeling.

"We are finished here Mr Rhodes, you are free to leave."

"As simple as that?"

"Yes Mr Rhodes, as simple as that. But we may need your cooperation again soon," replied Susan.

"Where do I go?" asked Leon.

"You need to get your belongings first. If you follow the officers who are waiting by the door they will take you to where you need to be."

Leon stood up and left the room. The officers by the door saw him and led him back to the holding sergeant where he retrieved his belongings. Once he was ready and had signed the necessary papers, he made his way out of the police station and headed for the nearest taxi rank. It was then he sensed someone following him. He turned onto a side street to see a shadow disappear behind some bins that was next to the loading bay for the Primark shop that led off this street. Leon realised he could be in danger so began to make his way back towards the entrance of the police station. When he was within ten feet of the door, he heard footsteps behind him. Leon turned just in time to see a flash of a blade come towards him. It took all his might to move inside and block the arm that held the blade. As he looked at the arm he now held he followed it down to the hand and saw that it was holding a samurai sword. He looked back up the arm to see that the person holding it was of far eastern descent and was wearing a very evil grin. Leon then saw the other arm arc towards him. He moved his other arm to block it and felt it connect with his assailant. As he did so he lifted his back leg, spun and executed a spinning back kick which connected with his assailants ribs. The person took a step back before screaming and making another lunge forward.

As the attacker screamed, Victor and Susan where making their way to the car to go and see some people regarding Leon's case when they heard the noise from the street beyond the walls. They looked round the exit gate of the police station to find Leon Rhodes desperately defending himself against an armed opponent with a sword. As they moved towards the scene, Leon's attacker sensed that there were people coming to his enemy's aid and decided that caution was the better part of valour.

As the attacker started to slide away, he said, "We will recover the secret that has been left for you as it is our belief that you are not worthy of the knowledge."

With that, the person disappeared into the side streets that led off from the police station. Leon could just see between a bin a silver car -Porsche, maybe- start up it's engine and speed away as Victor gave chase but he returned a few minutes later having unsuccessfully found the assailant.

Leon looked at Susan and said, "If you need proof of my innocence then that has just provided it!"

Susan looked at Victor who nodded before turning back to Leon, "It might be a good idea if you came back in the station and told us exactly what happened here."

* * * * * * * * * * * *

"All I did was walk out of the police station and then I was attacked," said Leon back in the interview room he had been in less than ten minutes ago. The only difference this time was that he was a victim of a crime rather than the suspect of one.

"The strange thing is, I got the feeling he was not an expert at what he was doing."

"What makes you think that?" asked Victor.

"He was holding the blade of the samurai called a Katana. They are supposed to sheath and unsheathe the sword before and after use as a sign of respect to their blade and they are to keep the blade in a good condition at all times. This blade was not in a good condition at all. The person using it held no belt with which to carry his katana. In fact, this person had no skill with the sword at all. He was merely holding it as a weapon. If they had been skilled at using that sword, I would not be here talking to you now. He was, however, skilled in other martial arts."

Victor sat for a moment before speaking, "Your assailant said something to you before he ran away. What did he say?"

"He said I was not worthy to hold the secret that has been left for me."

"There are constant references to a secret in Malcolm's diary. Could they be the same?" asked Susan.

"It's a possibility," began Victor, "I think we need to take Mr Rhodes here to where Malcolm Gaines body was found." Leon went pale at the thought of seeing the scene. Victor sensed his uneasiness at the idea, "Its OK, Mr Rhodes, Malcolm's body has been removed."

Leon looked at Victor, nodded then said, "Fine I'll go. But will you call me Leon please?"

The three of them got up from their chairs and made there way out of the interview room, through the police station and out a door that led to the car park. Victor led them to a black Vauxhall Astra which they all got in. He started the engine, made his way out of the car park and turned onto the ring road in the direction of the crime scene. Leon looked out of the window and wondered about the journey he was about to undertake.

Chapter nine

Shogun Shimazu of the Satsuma clan let out a bellow of rage from his chair as the leader of what remained of the raiding party he had sent to capture the small band of outlaws gave the bad news to him.

"You are useless!" he bellowed, "What am I to do? Apprehend them myself!"

"I am sorry, my lord," began the leader, "We tried to get there as quickly as we could, but they resisted harder than we had been led to believe."

"Silence! I do not want excuses," the leader sank even lower on his knees then he already was, "you are removed from duty. I do not tolerate failure."

Shimazu reached for his Katana, stood up and in one swift move buried the blade between the shoulder blades of the unfortunate man. He let out a brief moan of pain before going limp. *'I will not even let you have the honour of removing your head for such failure!'* The head of the prefecture removed the blade, wiped it clean on the attire of the now deceased man and sat back down while the rest of the raiding party removed their leader from the room.

An unseen presence from the shadows who had been watching the events in the throne room unfold, moved forward and addressed Shimazu, "The intended abduction of the protector was unsuccessful?"

"Yes it was. I take it you have a plan to over come this little problem?"

"The most logical plan now is to get to Shanghai before they do. I have contacts there which will prove useful. I believe the gifted one's cooperation is only a matter of time."

"For your sake, I hope it is," stated Shogun Shimazu, "I want those boxes. Do whatever it takes to get them. Do you understand me?"

"Perfectly, my Lord."

"You may take the fastest horse we have and I will arrange passage to China for you."

"Thank you, my Lord."

With that, the unseen person turned and exited Shimazu's room without anybody seeing them.

* * * * * * * * * * * *

The port of Naha was busy enough when the group of five arrived a day after setting out from Shuri. Over by a large sailing ship was a bunch of European sailors loading provisions. Shumi stared in wonder at them and realised that these strange looking people represented other places in the world that she had never dreamed of seeing.

Chojiro was staring round the port trying to get his bearings and find the ship that would give them safe passage. Unfortunately, Takahara had not told him the name of a ship only that safe passage had been organised. What could the ship be called? He knew the way his instructor thought and that he would have chosen a ship with an appropriate name but he couldn't think what name it would be.

"Where is this ship?" asked Jano.

"I don't know. Takahara san never got chance to tell me before we was attacked by the samurai," replied Chojiro.

"Oh great!" moaned Gogen. He had never stopped complaining since the moment they set out together. If the sun was too hot, then he was thirsty all the time. If he was hungry, he'd complain of a growling stomach. Chojiro thought this man was just born to complain, "Did you not think to ask the name of this ship before you brought us together?"

"I was being attacked by the samurai before I could ask. An answer may have been difficult to give from a man who was killed and then beheaded!" answered Chojiro, coolly.

"There must be someway of finding out which ship has been booked for us," interrupted Shumi, "perhaps we should go to each one and ask the captain if he has been contacted by Takahara san?"

"There are a lot of ships. I'd say there at least a hundred just docked. And then there will be the ones that will dock today and then there will be ships departing that we might never get chance to ask," explained Kosaku.

"He's right, Shumi," began Jano, "We need to narrow the search. Chojiro holds the answer; he just needs to figure it out."

'Jano is right,' thought Chojiro*, 'the answer is within me. But where do I start? What clues would my Instructor leave me?* "Let's go find somewhere to eat."

"At last, the first sensible thing to be said all day!" exclaimed Gogen.

They left dockside and headed into the town to find an eating hall. When they located a busy one just off the main walkway, they found a table and sat down. It wasn't too long before a server came over. They ordered, and before they knew it, there was bowls of rice on the table. The group ate ravenously for several minutes until their hunger was sated and they started to slow down. Chojiro had realised this was the first thing he had eaten in over a day. He hadn't quite realised how hungry he actually was.

"Where are you going to begin?" asked Kosaku.

"I don't know. My instructor always did things so that they were symbolic to himself and others. That's the only clue as to where we start," said Chojiro in between mouthfuls of rice.

"This venture is doomed," began Gogen, "if you can't figure the first problem out, I may as well go home."

"Shut up, Gogen," said Shumi irritably.

There was a pause as everybody ate and looked at each other for a clue as what to do next. All of a sudden, Chojiro stood, "I need to look at something. Jano, can you pay the girl for the meal if I'm not back soon?"

Jano nodded and went back to eating from his bowl.

Chojiro walked away from the rest of the group. His intention was to find a secluded spot and have a look at the boxes that were given to him. In the heat of all that happened yesterday he had not had time to inspect them properly and felt it was right to do so now. He just needed a little privacy.

He eventually found it by a clump of trees a little way from the dining hall. He went behind them and dropped to his knees. He reached inside his robes and pulled out the two boxes. He slid the first one open which had the key in it. It was small and black with no inscriptions or carvings on at all. '*No luck there then,*' thought Chojiro. He turned his attention to the red box, which he opened using the key from the first box. He had never noticed anything inside the box other than the Bubishi and now this time he was able to inspect it properly. The small book was laid upon a lining of finest silk. As Chojiro opened the lid fully he could see that the same fine silk was also sewn to the underside of the lid. He gave a small gasp when he saw what had been embroidered on the silk.

It was the picture of Fung Chi-Niang fending off the crane that was trying to steal her grain. It was the movements of the crane that inspired the formation of White crane Kung fu. This Chojiro knew because Takahara had taught him the history of many martial arts. He could see his mentor calling to him with the picture but he was unsure how. Disappointed in himself he locked the box back up, putting the key in the other and secreting the boxes back in his robes. He made his way back to the dining hall to find Jano paying the serving girl as he sat down.

"How did it go?" asked Kosaku.

"It cleared my head and has given me some ideas," Chojiro replied.

"You have ideas. Well, let's get started then," said Jano with renewed vigour.

"No wait," interrupted Gogen, "I want to know what those idea's are."

"I can't go into details. You will just have to trust me."

Gogen eyed Chojiro critically as though he was about to call him a liar, but before he could Shumi bounded past grabbing Chojiro and dragging him away. Everybody else got up and made to follow the leading two except Gogen who waited a couple of seconds as though deciding not to get up. He gave a sullen sigh before standing and following the rest of the group back to the port.

Chojiro realised he needed to think fast otherwise this journey was going to fall flat on its face before it had even got started. The picture he had seen on the box was a clue, but what did it tell him? As far as Chojiro could tell it was just a picture but he could sense a meaning in the picture just beyond his grasp. They walked round the docks looking this way and that but nothing came to him. They walked to one end of the port and still nothing jumped out at Chojiro. He could start to see boats make their way out to sea and be replaced by other ships which began unloading their cargo. They had made their way from one end of the port and were about to go to the other when Chojiro saw it. On the back of a boat was a sign from Takahara. A picture of the crane from the inside of the bubishi's box. Shumi could see that something had caught her husband's eye, "What is it, Chojiro?"

"I think I may have found our boat," he replied.

"Quick everybody, Chojiro has found it!"

"He's found it?" Gogen said, sounding almost disappointed.

"Will you stop being so negative," Kosaku began, "Chojiro has found the way. I had no doubt."

They all ran to the boat to find Chojiro looking round almost as though he was inspecting it. What he was doing was actually trying to confirm that this was the boat that Takahara had booked for them. He looked up to find the words confirming it for him. *The White Crane*. The name of this boat. 'Thank you, Sensei. You have led me well,' he thought.

From inside the boat, the captain could see this group of people looking at his boat. 'At last they are here. I was about to go without them.' He walked out onto the deck and shouted, "Is that you Takahara? You made no mention of five of you. You led me to believe it was yourself and one other!"

The name was right but it came as a surprise to him that this man was not expecting a large group. Chojiro needed to think quickly. He looked to his left to find Gogen, of all people, next to him. An idea rose in his mind, "Call to him Takahara san."

"I'm not Takahara...." Gogen's voice trailed off. He had quickly grasped what Chojiro was hinting at. "You can't be thinking what I am?"

Chojiro nodded. Gogen rolled his eyes as though pretending to be someone else was the most distaining thing that could be asked of him. "Yes it is me, Yahtsume Takahara! I'm sorry for the extra numbers. I would have notified you but it was a last minute thing."

"No, it's OK. I would have preferred some notice," as he walked towards the group before dropping a plank to allow them to jump on board, "but I have enough room for you all."

The group, except Kosaku came forward to engage the captain who shook hands with Gogen, "It is so kind of you to allow passage across the sea. May I introduce my friends..." He began to introduce the group and they were talking amongst themselves about the voyage they were to undertake.

Meanwhile Kosaku was looking back at the port taking in the sight of his home island for the last time in a while when he heard a commotion at the far end of the port. There was some screams and shouting as the crowd of people in the port began to part to allow some other people through who were being rather rough with them as they did so. As the commotion got nearer, Kosaku could see that it was a group of about twenty samurai heading from the town and coming in their direction. His eyes widened in fear at the approaching men. He walked back towards the boat and his friends never once taking his eyes off the approaching scene and tapped Chojiro on the shoulder. "Not now Kosaku. We are discussing our voyage here..." and turned back towards the captain to continue his conversation with him. Kosaku's tapping became more insistent.

"WHAT!" he barked and looked over his shoulder at Kosaku.

It was then that he noticed the approaching men and he tapped Gogen on his shoulder too. Gogen looked round himself to see the men coming towards them. He looked at Chojiro with a touch of fear in his face then turned towards the captain. "Perhaps we can continue this conversation once we have set off?" he said, a little more anxiously then he should.

"Sure. I want to get going as much you do."

With that he turned towards his boat and began untying the ropes which held it to the shore. The group ran aboard and began untying the other ropes as quickly as they could. The captain, not sensing the reason for his guests' sudden need for haste said, "Thank you. This will certainly speed up our departure," as he pulled on a rope which allowed the main sail to drop. He went into the small cabin at the rear and turned on the wheel of the boat. It turned picking up the wind and started to accelerate away from the port. The samurai were still a good couple of hundred yards from the place were their boat had been moored but were still giving chase. They finally made it to where they had once been and looked out towards the boat which was now about fifty yards away from them. Chojiro could see one of the samurai had lifted a bow and was about to take a shot at the boat when another man put his arm across him. The bow was lowered and the samurai continued to look on at the departing boat. After a while he could see them move away from the mooring and make their way back towards the town. '*To tell their leader no doubt,*" thought Chojiro. He turned to look at the rest of the group who where also beginning to relax and make themselves comfortable for the journey ahead of them.

A nagging doubt was forming at the back of his mind. Why was it the samurai turned up wherever he was? How did they know where to look every time? Something was amiss here and Chojiro was worried about it. It was well known that the Prefecture had spies every where but how did they know what was being done?

Questions were all that Chojiro had at the moment. Answers he would eventually get whether he wanted them or not.

As night began to fall, he looked out to sea and wondered what Shanghai had in store for him next.

Chapter ten

The Vauxhall Astra made its way up the drive towards the factory that Malcolm Gaines owned. It was mid afternoon and there was a slight breeze which was gently rustling the trees as they arrived. It was quite hot but not uncomfortable as the three people exited the car and made their way towards the entrance of the factory. As they went through the doors Leon could see the reason that Kenneth enjoyed his visits here. There was memorabilia of martial arts all over the place and Leon found it hard not to stop and look at a seven foot statue of a white crane that was situated just by the reception desk and everything else that was mounted or positioned around the entrance. They walked through to an area that was marble and stone with no markings whatsoever and found a button which Victor pressed. After a while some doors opened and allowed them access to the lift. When they got in Susan pressed the button which would take them to the top floor. As they arrived at the top floor they followed the corridor round to the right until they reached a big oak door. Victor pushed it open and Susan and Leon walked through. They were obviously walking to an area that was private within the building and not every employee of Malcolm's company had access to. As they entered the room there was a number of bookshelves that resembled a large private library and as Leon walked past he caught a look at the names of books. Malcolm Gaines had obviously compiled a large number of books with which to conduct his research, Leon wished the man was still alive so that he could petition the use of this library. It would certainly have helped his research. However this was of no concern to him right now as he made his way past it all and on to Malcolm's inner sanctuary and the place where he had been found murdered.

"How did you know that Malcolm had been murdered?" asked Leon.

"We received an anonymous tip," answered Victor.

"Did you not find it unusual?"

"Sure it was a little strange. The call placed to the switchboard had been a little too specific."

"How do you mean too specific?"

"Instead of someone saying he had seen somebody murdered, we received a call saying that they had seen Malcolm Gaines murdered."

Leon thought for a moment, "Surely that must have sent some alarm bells ringing?"

"It did. When we got here, we found the beheaded man and his diary plus a few other things which we didn't think were relevant at the time. However, the attack on you had begun to change things slightly. I don't know how but I think that's were your expertise will come in handy."

"What other things did you find?"

"If you wait a couple of minutes we'll show you," interrupted Susan.

As they reached the end of the library, they were met with a couple more large oak doors. Victor opened them to reveal Malcolm's inner sanctuary. Despite Malcolm's middle aged years the room was quite modern with black leather sofas and laminate flooring. On one wall there was a big plasma screen with a DVD and video players. To the side of this was many DVD's, all of which were martial arts based. Leon looked at the titles and recognised many that were in his collection. *'This man loved his Karate,'* thought Leon.

"As you can see, he was a follower of martial arts," said Susan, "his video collection is extensive. His research library is even more so."

"What is it you want me to see?" asked Leon.

"This was found on his desk by the diary. The page that was shown to you in the interview room was where the diary was found open. That was why we brought you in. We originally thought that this was a message from Malcolm naming his killer. However the attack on you outside the police station made us think differently," answered Susan as she handed a miniature sized statue of the white crane that stood at the reception desk.

Leon took it from Susan and looked at it. It was an exact copy. Its wings were spread out and its head was bent down as though it was about to take flight. He looked from the statue to the desk and thought about the connection between the two. Something was missing. There was the beginning of a puzzle that Malcolm had laid before them, but it felt like a piece was missing.

"Was there anything else found in here?" said Leon as he continued to look at the desk.

"There was also a piece of paper next to the statue but it was written in Chinese or oriental handwriting. Here," answered Susan as she rummaged through a folder which contained evidence from this scene.

Leon took it from her, looked at it and blew his cheeks out.

"What?" glared Victor.

"Malcolm has left a copy of a page of the Bubishi. Not just any page as well. This is one of the pages that Master Funakoshi published in his first book, look!"

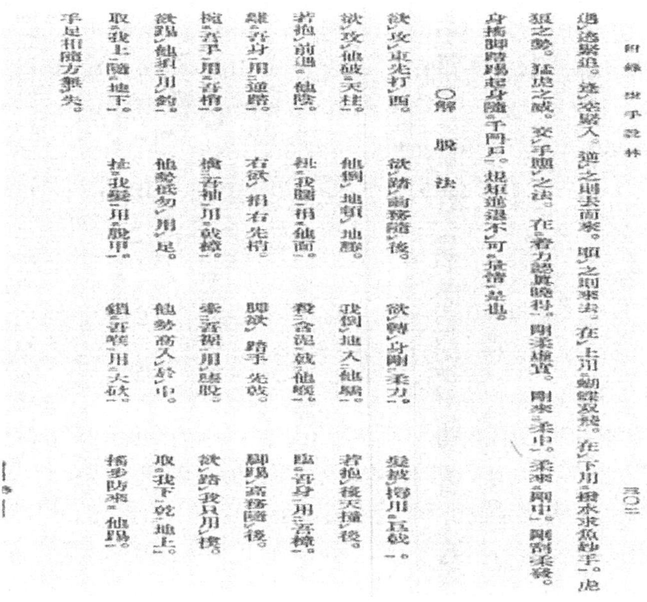

"It's pretty much unreadable, unless you know Chinese," finished Leon.

"So let me get this right," began Victor, "Malcolm Gaines left some clues to something. This begs a few questions. What is he trying to say? Why has he done this? Plus, he left these things out in a pretty ordered way. I would say that he expected this to happen. That was why we also thought of you. There is an entry in his diary with your meeting planned. There is also a note saying he was bringing his protector. As you can see there was evidence against you. However in the current light we think these clues where meant for you rather than to implicate you."

"I would agree but I don't see any meaning in all this," Leon said, "The diary is important because Malcolm probably wanted me to know his thoughts. The page of the Bubishi was done to reinforce the message to include me. The statue does not make sense."

"Yes, the statue is an odd one. Is there anything you can think of that might be able to help us here?" asked Victor.

"It's the same as the one in the reception area."

"Yes, we noticed that too," Victor said, "an exact replica. But there is nothing else on either statue."

It was at times like this that Leon thought of Kenneth. He usually provided some sort of insight that proved helpful or solved whatever was on Leon's mind. He decided that this was the time for Ken's intervention.

"Can I use your phone?"

Susan intervened, handing her mobile phone over to Leon, "Use mine," she said.

He dialled the number and waited. It rang once, twice, three times. On the forth ring Kenneth answered, "Hello."

"Ken it's me."

"Ah yes, Leon. I was wondering when you might ring. Has our local constabulary finally decided that you are no longer the focus of their enquiries?"

"Sort of, I'm no longer the suspect if that's what you mean."

"Good, how can I help you then?"

"Could you come to Malcolm's factory?"

"Sure. I'll be there in ten minutes."

"Thanks Ken," Leon switched off the phone and handed it back to Susan, "he will be here in ten minutes. Until then let's look at this stuff again."

* * * * * * * * * * * * *

Ken walked through the doors to Malcolm's office fifteen minutes later and looked round in awe at the scene that was in front of him. He had never been this far in before and let out an appreciative whistle when he came to the waiting group.

"Now then lad, what did you call me here for?" Ken asked.

Leon walked forward and let out a relaxed smile that let Ken know that he was no longer in this situation because the police had forced him to, "I was hoping we would be able to benefit from one of your unique insights."

"Well let's have a look then."

Leon led Ken over to the desk and motioned towards the three clues that had been left for him. Ken surveyed the desk before sitting on the chair in front of it and looking closely at the evidence in front of him. He picked up the piece of paper with the excerpt from the Bubishi on it.

"Somebody wanted your attention here," as Ken motioned to the piece of paper.

"I know. That's what I thought too."

Ken picked up the diary and looked at it, "I'd say he wanted you to know his thoughts, in fact...." Kens voice trailed off as he started to think. Leon looked on as his friend, trainer and mentor began to formulate ideas that always led somewhere new and thought provoking.

"Yes?" asked Victor.

"The diary is the key. He didn't just want you to know his thoughts. Clues to your journey are here in this book."

"Journey?" said Leon, perplexed, "I didn't ask to go on a journey."

"All the same, one has been laid before you," replied Ken.

This was not making any sense to Victor. He felt like he was listening in on a private conversation.

"Are you telling me that some sort of treasure hunt is behind all this?" he asked.

Ken turned to Victor, "There is more to this story. Malcolm was protecting a secret and I've known for some time. I gave him the space to learn what it was, but when I thought it was my time to learn it, his reply was 'when you are worthy of the knowledge', which I thought was a little selfish. But I didn't think for one second that this was a secret somebody thought it was worth killing for."

"Exactly how far can we expect to go on this journey?" asked Leon.

"I don't know, Karate is a life long journey, but you don't travel far from your own home," Ken replied, sagely

"What else do you know here, Ken?" interrupted Susan, keen not to stray too far from the matter at hand.

"I'm prepared to bet there is a reference to the statue in this diary," said Ken who came out of the reverie about his old friend Malcolm and started to rifle through the book. The other three waited in silence while he did so.

After about five minutes of looking Ken apparently found what he thought might be something, "Here, I think I might have it. Listen," he began to read, "This figure is part of the protector. Only the worthy will make the connection. If they do, the first step to acquiring knowledge is the beginning of their quest."

"Are you sure this could be it?" asked Leon examining the page offered to him by Ken.

"There are drawings of the figure here. Dimensions, materials, everything."

"It's an exact replica of the one in the reception," answered Victor.

Ken began absentmindedly playing with the figure as though trying to open its secrets.

"There must be some connection between the two..." Susan's voice trailed off as she looked at Ken. He had managed to twist the figure on its base.

As they looked at the figure more closely, Ken's twisting had revealed an opening in the base.

"What's inside, Ken?" asked Leon.

Ken stuck his little finger in, "Nothing," he replied.

Victor took one look at the pair of them and smiled for the first time since Leon had met him, "I'm surprised the pair of you haven't made the connection yet considering Malcolm Gaines thought one of you worthy of his secret."

"You what?" Ken said.

"Two statues, one big one small, you managed to twist the small one. Stands to reason the same could be done with the big one."

Leon smiled realising what Victor was getting at, " That's the first sensible comment you have made to me today!" With that, Leon turned and made his way back towards the lift. Victor, Susan and Ken quickly followed.

They all entered the lift and when it had made its way to the ground floor they exited and made their way to the large statue in the reception area. When they arrived, they all looked at it and began to weigh up its size and weight, preparing themselves for the big heave.

"I don't know, it looks pretty heavy," said Susan.

"Nonsense love, Leon and I have been known to push much heavier weights," Ken answered.

Leon looked dubiously at Ken reminding himself to ask when they had done because he couldn't remember. However, now was not the time.

"Right, two each on the wings. Leon and myself on the outside of the left wing and you two on the inside of the right. Are we ready? After three. One, two, THREE!" shouted Ken.

Everybody heaved, pushed, grunted and tried everything they could to twist the statue. It would not budge. After they all got their breath back, they tried again. It still would not move.

"If Malcolm was to do this on his own, his secret would be very safe. No one can get into it," rasped Susan, realising the cigarette she had in the car on the way here was not a good idea.

"No, he would have a way to get to it without the help of anyone else," gasped Leon.

Despite his heavy breathing, Victor looked at the statue before walking round it and saw the answer to this problem. He let out a laugh.

"Come look at this!"

The other three made their way to Victor. Ken looked down and let out a chuckle himself.

"If I knew it was going to be that easy, I wouldn't have been so quick to use muscle."

Susan bent down, put the plug into the socket and pressed the button a little higher up. As she did so, the statue began to make a rumbling noise before starting to twist revealing an open panel in the same way the miniature model did. Susan reached inside and pulled out a small bundle wrapped in a plain cloth. She opened the package to reveal a box with a button to press to unclasp it. She pressed the button and opened the box. Inside was a key which was long and narrow. At one end it had the normal circular handle and at the other it just had a few protrusions from the main shaft of the key.

"Looks like a safe key. I should know as I have one similar at the academy," mentioned Ken

"Where's the safe it opens?" asked Susan.

"Let's consult the diary," Ken answered.

Ken opened the diary back at the page he had found earlier and read the passage again.

"The only thing that makes any sense is the bit about acquiring knowledge," he said.

This time it was Leon who smiled after making a connection.

"Name me a place where people gain knowledge."

Susan answered, "I don't know, a college, a school, a library."

Ken caught the thread.

"An academy!"

"Yes, an academy!" as Leon nodded.

"Did he have one?" asked Victor.

"Not quite," said Ken, "in true Malcolm Gaines style he paid for one. I know exactly where it is. It's also appropriately named, considering everything before us tonight. It's called The White Crane Academy and it's not far from here in Netherthwaite."

Susan stuffed the diary and the small figure back in to her evidence folder before following the other three to the Astra that was still parked in front of the reception doors. Victor gunned the engine as the other three got in to the car and they sped off in the direction of Netherthwaite village.

If they had been more observant, they would have noticed a grey Porsche Carrera waiting and watching the factory. As they left, its engine revved up and the car began to follow from a discreet distance. Inside, its occupant pressed a button on his mobile phone bringing it into life from its hands-free socket. The phone rang five times before it was answered. He waited for the network's automated message to finish.

"It has begun," replied the occupant after the end of the beep. His voice had an oriental accent but he had been taught English from a young age. The English was perfect but he had never lost the effect of his native language.

There was no continuation with the message. The oriental man hung up the phone and continued to follow the black Astra from a distance.

* * * * * * * * * * * *

Victor turned the car into the car park of the white crane academy fifteen minutes later. After switching off the engine they all got out and surveyed the scene before them. The building itself was fairly new and modern with double glazing throughout. The entrance could be made by walking towards a couple of glass panels which slid open once you got anywhere near them.

"Whatever happened to good old fashioned door handles," commented Ken.

Susan rolled her eyes, while Leon just smiled. Ken always wanted the best for their academy but whenever he encountered something which they could not compete with he had to belittle it as much as possible.

Victor led the way towards the dojo and was looking around in the hope that they might meet somebody, but there appeared to be no one whatsoever. They continued along the corridor passing changing rooms, weights rooms and even a sauna and Jacuzzi room until they saw a door at the end with a sign on it saying '*Dojo*'. Victor peered through it to see it was empty too. He pushed the door handle down and it opened to reveal a state of the art training area. There were punch bags along one side, while on the other there was one long wall full of shelving where kick pads and punch pads where neatly stacked as well as medicine balls of all weights and sizes and dumbbells of all weights too. At the far end was one full length mirror which stretched along the entire wall. Leon thought that this must be the most equipped Dojo he had ever seen.

As they walked across the Dojo, they could see a door leading from the training area. It was labelled '*offices*'. The group made towards it until it opened and revealed a person in traditional white gi top but black training pants. He closed the door behind him before turning and seeing four people stood before him. If this alarmed him he did not show it. He merely smiled warmly and asked, "Can I help you?"

Ken walked forward and held his hand out, "my name is Ken Barrett, Chief instructor of the Helme valley black belt academy. This is my fellow instructor Leon Rhodes. The other two are police officers."

The man's smile faded at the mention of the police, "Pleased to meet you..."

"Victor Ugiagbe."

"Susan Jones"

"Yes, Victor and Susan. How can I be of assistance?"

"We were hoping we might be able to see Malcolm's office," said Victor taking the lead.

"I'm afraid not. You'll need to catch Mr. Gaines when he's in but he hasn't been here since last week when he trained," replied the instructor.

"I'm afraid he was found dead last night," answered Victor.

The instructors eyes flew wide open in shock, "Dead?! But I only spoke to him the day before last. I....I..." His words failed him.

"It's OK," soothed Susan, "I know this must come as a shock to you, but perhaps if you just told my colleagues the way, you would be helping us in our investigation."

"Last door at the end of the corridor, you can't miss it," he pointed sadly at the door he had just exited. As Leon, Victor and Ken turned towards it; Susan put her arm round the shocked and dejected instructor and led him towards the other end of the Dojo where there were a few seats. Victor turned back round and caught Susan's eye. She nodded before returning to the now quietly sobbing instructor as Leon opened the door and held it for the others to follow.

As it shut behind them, Ken grumbled, "don't know why he's so upset. I'm sure Malcolm's will leaves them set up for life."

Secretly, Leon agreed but he didn't comment as they approached the door to Malcolm's other office. He stepped forward and pushed the door open. As he peered round, he could see that the room was empty and moved to enter completely. The other two followed and started to search for a safe. Leon went to the desk and began to look around it hoping to find something. After a while they didn't find a thing.

"I'm sure this is the right place," said Ken.

"So am I," mused Leon. Just as he was about to give up, he looked down from the chair he was sitting on. Waiting to be found was a carpet square framed by a plastic boarder which, when the piece was removed, revealed a safe cutting into the floor. Leon took the key that Susan had given to him in the car on the trip over there and inserted it into the safe. He twisted the key, turned the central dial until he heard a clunk and opened the safe door. Inside were a black box and a slightly larger red box. Leon fished them out of the safe and put them down on the desk to look at. He was about to open the black box when Ken stopped him. "Not here lad. Let's wait until we are somewhere safe. This might be the reason that someone killed Malcolm. We're sitting targets, so let's just get out of here."

Victor nodded in agreement, "This could be crucial to the investigation, we'll head back to the station were it is safe."

Leon put the boxes in each of the inside pockets of his black blazer jacket and followed Victor and Ken out the door, when all of a sudden Victor's radio crackled to life, "Vic, you there?"

"Yes Sue, what's the matter?" replied Victor.

"There's someone here to see Leon."

"Right, we'll be there in a minute," said Victor as he clicked off the radio, "I suggest you keep those boxes out of sight. The reason Malcolm was killed may be waiting just beyond those doors."

"I hope not," said Leon, "but let's go and find out."

The three men started to run towards the door.

* * * * * * * * * * * * *

"There's someone here to see Leon," said Susan before handing the walkie-talkie back to the man stood opposite her. He simply nodded, smiled and hit her square across the jaw, knocking her clean out. Susan crumpled to the floor next to the instructor who had attempted to defend them both as the oriental man entered the room. He had been no match for him and was easily dispatched. After getting Susan to perform an important duty, he needed her out of the way too. *'One less to worry about.'* He turned to see three men enter the room.

"What on earth has happened here?" asked Victor, gesticulating towards the two prone figures of Susan and the instructor.

The assailant said nothing but started to walk towards the three of them with a menacing glint in his eye.

"I don't think this man is here to give an explanation," said Ken, who moved towards him quickly followed by Leon

"Stay out of this Victor. Make your way to Susan and the instructor and try to get them out of here."

Victor nodded and held back. After a while he started to make his way round the edge of the Dojo and watched the scene unfold.

The man attacked Ken by jumping up and performing a flying side kick. Ken saw it coming and twisted his body around and down. Leon walked forward and attacked the man while he was just coming down from the kick. He expertly fended it away and launched a blistering set of punches at Leon who fended most of them off but they came at him so fast a few hit their target. Ken intervened to allow Leon to move away and engage him close up which was his strength. Once, twice, three times Ken hit the man with devastating uppercuts before tying the man down onto the floor and putting him into an arm bar. The man arched his back to lessen the effects of the hold. After taking breath for a few seconds he lifted his legs into the air with supreme strength and rolled over his shoulders twisting Ken with him. He broke free of the hold, stood up and was about launch a devastating hammer fist to Ken's exposed neck when Leon intervened and blocked the move with an eskrima stick he had found on the shelving in the Dojo. The man recoiled in pain. It hurts when that happens!

He barely had time to recover from the pain when Leon attacked him with swift moves that left the man in no way able to defend himself. Several times Leon caught him with blows across the face and the welts were beginning to show. With the final blows Leon hit him with a mid range blow that caught him flush in the ribs, there was a cracking noise, a cry of pain and the man went to the floor where he stayed.

Leon, breathing hard, dropped the sticks and turned to Ken who was just getting up from the floor. He held his hand out to him and helped Ken up as he took his hand. They both turned to look at Victor who was helping a groggy Susan to a seating position on the floor.

"Everything OK, Victor?" Leon asked

"Yes, they are both coming round now," Victor said.

Satisfied that they were indeed fine, Leon and Ken turned towards their prostrate attacker. They could see he was still conscious and breathing heavy while holding his ribs. The man had turned away from them and trying to heave himself to his feet. Ken came forward and put his hand on the man's shoulder.

"I don't think you are going anywhere pal!"

As Ken finished his sentence Leon saw a glint of metal, "No!" he shouted as he saw Ken take a small blade straight to his calf.

Ken collapsed in pain as the blade sliced through the muscle, spewing blood all over the dojo floor. Leon ran towards the man and Ken but it was too late. Ken's attacker had already begun to make his way out of the Dojo. Leon didn't care anymore. He knelt beside Ken, "are you alright?"

"Course I am lad!" screamed Ken through the pain, "don't worry about me, just get after the twat!"

Leon stood and sprinted after the assailant. As he ran along, he saw his quarry just disappearing through the automatic doors. He ran as fast as he could towards them and as he got through, he looked around and saw a Porsche Carrera starting up. He knew he wasn't going to get to the car in time but instead ran towards the exit of the car park. As the Porsche turned and made its way towards the road, Leon had drawn parallel with the it. *'Thank God it's a convertible'* thought Leon as he made a desperate dive. He caught it on the rear window sill and somehow managed to haul himself in. He moved forward just as the oriental man noticed him. Leon let rip a range of punches at the driver. With only one hand defending a few got through and as each one connected the car veered off the road every now and again. The driver switched on the cruise control before changing position by hoisting his legs up onto the steering wheel while still defending himself from Leon's blows. This continued for a couple of miles. Many pedestrians watched in surprise at the scene that flew past them at sixty miles an hour. The driver tried to get Leon into an arm lock which he only just managed to get out of. Leon went to attack the legs but the driver launched a volley of punches catching him in the ribs. Then the driver continued to punch at Leon's face, which he defended away. The combat continued in this stalemate until a tight bend in the road approached. Leon attacked the driver who this time turned his body away. This caused his feet to turn the car hard to the right. Leon had to stop the attack just to regain his balance. As he did so, Leon's enemy had an idea. He quickly turned the car hard to the right and Leon lost his balance again. This caused Leon to fall forward grabbing at anything he could lay his hands on to regain his balance. This turned out to be a leather wallet that had been moving left and right on the dashboard as the car weaved. The car then lurched left straight after, causing Leon to stand hard up with his hands out stretched trying furiously not to fall out the car. As he did so, the driver let rip with a simple, but effective front kick, his heel catching Leon straight in the face. Then all of a sudden, the driver regained control of his Porsche and navigated the corner. This caused Leon to fly through the air and he was glad to see that beyond the tight corner was bushes which cushioned his fall and he landed slightly scratched and bleeding with a thump at the bottom of them. When he had climbed out and looked down the road, he could see the Porsche disappearing into the distance. The fact that he had lost a fight bothered him less when he took a look at the contents of the leather card wallet he realised was still in his hand.

* * * * * * * * * * * * *

Leon was picked up ten minutes later by a police car on the look out and it quickly deposited him back at the white crane academy. He was soon in the Dojo explaining what happened.

Ken smirked, "Your balance never was one of your strong points."

"Thanks!" said Leon in a sarcastic manner, "Lets get those boxes, take them to Malcolm's office and have a look. I want to see what all this fuss is about."

With that, Leon, Victor, Susan and a heavily limping and bandaged Ken went back to the office and sat around the desk while Leon opened the black box. In it was a key which looked the right size to open the red box. He pushed the first box to one side, turned his attention to the red one and inserted the key. As he twisted, the box made a slight click and waited to be opened fully. Leon let go of the key and moved his hands to the lid of the box and fully opened it. When he looked inside all he saw was a bunch of papers and Leon picked them up wondering what was so important. As he started to look through them, he caught sight of a page he had seen earlier today and when he did, he realised the significance of what he was holding.

"Oh my God, Ken take a look at this!"

Ken moved over and bent down over Leon's shoulder.

"Well I never. This is amazing!"

"What is it?" asked Victor, the suspense getting the better of him

"It's the Bubishi!" replied Leon.

"Not just any version," continued Ken, "it looks to be original considering the state it."

"This Bubishi is what exactly?" said Victor.

"A notebook for martial artists from very early times," replied Leon lost in what he was looking at, "it is supposed to be a precursor for all empty handed styles that originated from Okinawa. It's where all karate styles are thought to originate from."

Victor pondered for a moment, "How on earth does that fit into everything that has happened here?"

"I don't know Victor," began Leon, "but this is what Malcolm Gaines has left for us. I think we need to find out what he wanted us to do with it because we all continue to be in danger while the Bubishi is out in the open."

"Fair enough," shrugged Victor as he reached into Susan's evidence file and retrieved Malcolm's diary, "You've started this journey, I suggest you finish it. Hopefully it might help us to uncover Malcolm's killers so I hope you don't mind us tagging along?"

"Even if it takes us to the other side of the world," added Susan.

Leon suspected that promise might not be necessary.

Chapter eleven

Chojiro looked out over the rolling sea around him and felt a peace of mind that he had not known for a long time. The struggle against the Japanese was a world away from him now and he couldn't be more thankful. Shumi was safe with him and so were his friends, although Gogen was a worry. Why exactly was he with Jano that night? He's not even a member of the brotherhood so how did he know to go to Jano? These were questions Chojiro needed answers from if he was continuing this quest.

He had said it. A quest was what they had now embarked upon and Chojiro vowed silently and to himself to finish it. All he wanted was a quiet life with Shumi. He had begun to grow tired of the struggle and although he would never admit it to anyone else, he had thought about leaving it all behind before this task had been given to him.

Just then Shumi walked over to him and stood by his side looking out to sea. There was a long pause with the two of them looking before Shumi linked arms with Chojiro and turned him away from the scene before them. As they walked towards the stern of the boat, Chojiro remembered something, "Jano said that I needed to speak with you. He said you had some news for me."

Shumi stopped in her tracks, "I didn't think he had time to tell you. Your meeting was very short."

"I know. But he did seem very pleased to tell me the news. What exactly did you tell him? What is so important that I need to know after him?"

Shumi turned away from him before saying, "what I am about to tell you will change our lives forever, Chojiro. I am pregnant!"

Chojiro looked at his wife in a way he had never used before.

"You don't have to be happy, or pleased," she began, "in fact you don't have to think anything at all. I know how much this journey means to you."

"It means a lot to me Shumi," started Chojiro, "but not as much as the news you have just given me," a smile had begun to spread across his face.

At that moment Jano joined them, "I take it Shumi has told you the news. You are taking it exactly as I thought you would."

"I am absolutely delighted, Jano. I can't believe this is happening, but..." A cloud descended upon Chojiro.

"I know what you are thinking, Chojiro, Shumi cannot continue our journey. I have put into place plans for her to be looked after once we get to Shanghai. I have friends there and she will be perfectly safe until we have finished," said Jano.

A wave of appreciation overcame Chojiro as he hugged his wife before turning to Jano, "I am forever in your debt, my friend."

Jano nodded before turning and walking back towards the stern of the ship.

* * * * * * * * * * * *

"I'm telling you this journey is doomed to failure," said Gogen, "In fact, when we get to Shanghai I'm staying on this boat while it loads up, head back to Okinawa and to a safe life I enjoyed in the first place."

"You have no faith, Gogen."

"That maybe so Kosaku, But I am a realist. I do not expect us to get any further than the edges of Shanghai before we are all mercilessly slaughtered."

"What makes you think that?"

"You saw the way the Satsuma clan were able to find us so quickly. What is there to stop them using their allies to do the same in Shanghai?"

"We evaded them back home. I believe we can do the same over there," replied Kosaku.

"Does it not worry you that they were able to find us so easily?" asked Gogen.

"It does. But for the time being we are all safe. The sneak will show himself eventually. When he does, we will be ready."

Gogen eyed Kosaku critically before adding, "I never mentioned anything about a sneak amongst us"

Kosaku blushed and tried not to look at Gogen.

Chapter twelve

It was well into the evening as the four of them walked away from the White crane dojo to the awaiting black Astra. Leon mused to himself that the day was not planning out as he had hoped. He had gone from sleeping to a police cell, to factory, to dojo, to fighting in a car, then been kicked out of it into bushes and then had the Bubishi revealed to him. Not an ordinary day by any means.

Ken had appreciated what Leon was thinking when he said, "Not your average day is it?"

Leon smiled before getting in the back seat of the Astra. He didn't say another word until he got back to the police station despite Ken, Victor and Susan all debating their potential next step. There was a nagging doubt in Leon's mind which was preventing him from joining in their debate. He knew he had to confide in Ken the reality of what he thought after everything that had happened in the past few hours but unfortunately the opportunity never presented itself. Leon decided that he would have to bide his time and wait for the appropriate moment. Despite this, the thoughts that he had, never strayed far from his mind, even when they returned to the police station. Eventually Ken and Leon where led to another interview room. Susan started to empty the file that she was carrying while Victor went for a dry wipe whiteboard and some pens. He returned five minutes later to find Susan organising the evidence they had, Ken looking in the diary and Leon looking out of a window.

"What do we have so far, Susan?" he asked.

"We have the figure of the crane, the diary, the Bubishi with its two boxes, the key we found in the larger crane statue and the excerpt of the Bubishi found in Malcolm's office," recounted Susan.

"What is the next step, then?"

"There's nothing in the diary," said Ken.

"Could the clues point towards some other statue like the crane in the factory?" asked Susan.

"Do you know of any other crane statue round here?" questioned Victor looking at Ken who quickly shook his head.

All three of them turned to look at Leon who was still silent from the journey back to the police station. He finally noticed they were all waiting for him to say something.

"I have an idea," he began, "but I need to research it."

"What is it, Leon?" enquired Ken.

"Something you said earlier in Malcolm's office. A journey."

"A journey to where?"

"I don't know, Ken. That's why I need to do some research. I need to get on the internet and start looking."

"You can use the computers here at the station," said Victor.

"Actually, I would like to go home. I need a break, a shower and to be in a place I find comfortable. No offence," mumbled Leon.

"None taken," smiled Victor, "we could all use a break. Can you come back tomorrow at nine AM?"

Leon and Ken both nodded. Victor noted that Leon looked especially tired.

"Good. Get your thinking caps on. Let's sleep on it tonight and start with a fresh pair of eyes in the morning."

As Leon and Ken stood up Victor did the same, went to the door and held it open for them. He gave a smile that only Ken returned. When they had left the room, Victor turned to Susan and asked, "Is it me, or does Leon know something he's not telling us?"

Susan nodded in agreement.

* * * * * * * * * * * *

"Do you mind telling me what the hell was up with you back there?!" shouted Ken as he and Leon crossed the road to the taxi rank outside the police station.

"I don't trust them at the moment."

"Why would you not trust them?"

Leon did not answer but held his hand out for a taxi as one came near. It stopped for him and as Leon climbed in, he said, "Do you want dropping off?"

"Sure, but can you fill me in as to what you are thinking."

Ken sat down next to Leon who said to the taxi driver, "Linthwaite, please!"

Leon said nothing and kept looking forward, but he could tell that Ken was wearing an expression that said he did not like been kept in the dark for too long. After the police station was well out of sight, Leon looked over at Ken and handed him the leather wallet he had grabbed from the Porsche earlier in the day. As Ken opened it, he saw the very thing that Leon had seen. The reason that his friend had been cagey around Victor and Susan became immediately apparent.

"What on earth was that guy who attacked us doing with this in his wallet?" as he handed it back.

"I don't know, Ken."

Leon looked down at the West Yorkshire police constabulary badge and wondered exactly what he had let himself in for.

The rest of the taxi journey was made in complete silence before the taxi arrived at Ken's home.

"Do I owe you anything for the taxi?" he asked

"No Ken, I've got this. Are you on the computer later?"

"As you've said, we need to do some research."

"Speak to you later, then."

As the taxi drove off, Ken looked after it and wondered exactly what they were all going to have to do before this journey was through. He gave a worried sigh before he turned towards his house, rummaged in his pocket for his door key before putting it in the lock of his front door, turning it and entering his house. His wife had gone to bed and the house was dark. He walked through to his kitchen and switched on the lights. There was a note on the kitchen table from his wife saying that she had left some dinner in the fridge for him and that she hoped Leon was not in too much trouble with the police. Ken walked over to the fridge and looked in it. He decided he wasn't hungry and instead picked out the bottle of wine he was going to have with dinner that night. His wife had not touched it and it remained unopened. He went over to the cupboard next to the sink and retrieved the largest wine glass he could find. Next he located the corkscrew from a drawer and opened the bottle of wine. With his brain still buzzing from the events of the day he switched off the lights in the kitchen, walked into the living room, stopping only to touch the lamp next to the computer at the back of the room and sat down in front of it. He pressed the 'on' button and waited for it to start up. After a couple of minutes it asked which person was logging on to the computer. Ken took the mouse and pointed it over the picture next to his name. The icon highlighted itself and eventually Ken's desktop was on the screen. When it had done that, his messenger started to automatically load. It showed all his contacts off-line, including Leon. All of a sudden, another box appeared saying, '*friendofdaruma@hotmail.co.uk* has added you to his/her contact list. Do you wish to allow them to see when you are on-line and to allow them to contact you?' Underneath was two buttons one saying 'yes' the other 'no'.

Ken read the message before saying out loud, "Who the hell is this friend of Daruma?"

* * * * * * * * * * * *

Leon looked out at Ken as the taxi left and wondered what exactly his friend was thinking. He realised that an opportunity to tell Ken what he was really thinking had passed him by after he had shown him the badge of a policeman who had attacked him and yet they were working with two police officers of the same constabulary that was apparently trying to help them. As to what end, Leon did not know but he was determined to find out. After ten minutes, the taxi arrived at its destination; he paid the driver and made his way into his house. He went straight to his fridge and located a bottle of corona and went over to the fruit bowl where he found a lime, cutting a wedge out of it before opening the bottle of beer and sticking it in the top of the bottle. He made his way over to the computer in his living room, switched it on and waited a moment while it started before it asked for which person wanted to log on. He clicked on his own name and waited for his desk top to load up. When it did so it started to log on to his messenger. When it had loaded, Leon's messenger came up with a dialogue box saying, 'friendofdaruma@hotmail.co.uk has added you to his/her contact list. Do you wish to allow them to see when you are on-line and to allow them to contact you?' Intrigued Leon clicked the yes button. He received a message a few minutes later saying 'Hello Leon.'

Leon typed a reply, 'Who the hell are you?'

'A friend who wishes to help. Are you not sure what to do next?'

'I have an idea. Do you?'

'You have been trusted with a secret that needs to be kept safe.'

Leon pondered for a moment before typing, 'No journey to the other side of world then?'

'Not unless you wish to follow the Bubishi's original journey.' came the reply.

'Where will that take me?'

'On a futile pursuit of honour that did not work the last time.'

Leon looked at the last words and realised what he had to say to Victor, Susan and Ken tomorrow.

* * * * * * * * * * * * *

"You've decided to do what?" exclaimed Victor.

"I've decided to find a place to hide the Bubishi and make sure that it never comes to harm or falls into the wrong hands. Malcolm left this for me because he expects me to do what I'm intending," Leon replied.

"But what about finding the person who murdered Malcolm?" asked Susan.

Leon turned from facing Victor to answer Susan, "You don't need the Bubishi to do that. I'm still willing to help with this investigation in any way I can. But this has been given to me to protect and I must do so."

"But this book involves a journey, Ken and Malcolm said so." She countered.

"Only if I want it to. There is no obligation for me to undertake it. This book has remained hidden for a long time and it has been safe. Now it is in the open and it's never been in more danger. I want to get this book to safety where only I and a select few know where it is. Until then I can't help you."

When Leon had finished speaking he turned away from the assembled group and looked into the mirror of the interview room they were in. It wasn't until then that he realised they were in the same room when he was first questioned by Victor and Susan.

Victor, who could not believe what he was hearing, looked at Ken before asking, "Do you agree with what he is saying?"

Ken, who had been filled in with the previous night's events after Leon had picked him up in a taxi from his house on the way to the police station that morning, stated, "I agree with his reasons. However, I think he should continue to help even while he is trying to find his ingenious hiding place for the Bubishi."

Leon suppressed a small smile. He knew Ken would back him up, even as it turned out that Ken had pressed the 'no' button last night and missed joining the conversation Leon had on the computer.

Victor was now getting angry, "Do you have any idea what you are doing here?"

"Yes," answered Leon, "I know exactly what I am doing. I am guarding everybody's safety. There are very dangerous people after the Bubishi. What they want with it, I don't know. The only journey I'm now going to take is to the place that I have decided is going to become this book's *ingenious hiding place*." An even bigger smile spread across his face as he looked at Ken who smiled back.

"I'm sorry," added Leon, "when I am satisfied that the Bubishi is safe then I will contact you and if you still want me, I'll continue to help in your enquires regarding Malcolm's murder."

Victor and Susan said nothing in reply.

Having said everything he had wanted to, Leon motioned to Ken and they made their way out of the interview room. He picked up the Bubishi boxes, the excerpt and the diary, placing the boxes in his inside pocket and the excerpt and diary into a file he found lying on a table as they walked out.

After a minute had passed, Victor finally said, "I'd better go and inform the boss."

He made his way out of the interview room, leaving Susan to tidy up what little evidence they had, and made his way up a flight of stairs. When he got to the top, he opened the door to his left and walked onto a corridor. He continued further for a few yards and stopped at a door before knocking. He waited for the occupant to say 'Enter!', and walked into the room.

Chief Inspector John Hadrian looked up expectantly as Victor entered. He sat down at the chair in front of his desk before letting out a deep sigh.

Hadrian began, "Have you come to give me some good news, Detective?"

"I'm afraid not. Leon Rhodes has decided not to help us with our investigation for the time being," answered Victor.

"Why?"

"He feels that to continue would put everyone concerned in danger."

"This is most unsatisfactory, Victor."

"I know. Leon feels that Malcolm entrusted the boxes to him to protect, not to uncover a secret we are not even sure is there. I feel that to continue what we were doing was going to draw in whoever killed Malcolm Gaines."

"I agree, Victor. The question is how do we get Mr Rhodes back into the investigation?"

"There is nothing I can do. He said he will contact us when he is ready to rejoin the investigation. He feels he needs to make sure this Bubishi is safe first."

Hadrian did not reply. He merely drummed his fingers on the desk looking straight at Victor without once losing eye contact with him.

After a while, he looked as though he had made his mind up about something, but what that was Victor could not tell. "Very well. Thank you for keeping me informed on events. Please continue with your investigation." Victor stood and began to make his way towards the door. "One last thing."

"Yes Chief?"

"Leon Rhodes knows something we do not. Until you find out what that is he will not help in this investigation. However, he will return sooner or later. Let's see if we can make it sooner."

Victor nodded and left the room.

* * * * * * * * * * * *

"I thought he took that better than we feared," began Ken, "in fact, he was almost glad we were leaving the investigation!"

Leon leered disbelievingly at his friend before getting into his car. After a moment he decided to ask a question that had been on his mind since the incident at the White crane dojo.

"Why has uncovering the Bubishi caused people to come after us Ken?"

"By people you mean one person."

"No, I was attacked outside the police station. But why did the guy at the dojo go straight for us, he had never seen us before yesterday."

"I haven't a clue, Leon. But we have the only means of finding out."

"What do you mean?"

"The diary, lad." Ken reached into the file, pulled out the diary, removing the loose notes which he put back in the file and began to skim through it.

True, thought Leon, "but surely Malcolm must have found out the real reason behind the Bubishi?"

"He might not have done so. Or the Bubishi is just an historical document that some collector really wants to get hold of."

Leon had never considered the possibility of really persistent antique hunters before. The more he thought about it, the less likely it seemed.

It was Ken's turn to think for a second, The real reason behind the Bubishi? Are you telling me there is more to it then just an instruction manual?

Now was the time for Leon to tell Ken what he had been hiding from his friend for some time, "The research for the book I conducted away from you uncovered some interesting writings, most noticeably on the internet. The majority were conspiracy theory rubbish. I particularly enjoyed the one that said the authorities were trying to get hold of it to learn the teachings and techniques so as to create super policemen. But one or two were quite sane and sensible. The most intriguing was that the Bubishi holds a secret so powerful that if any man was to seriously study certain principles and techniques, they would have the power of life and death over others."

These words were proving hard for Ken to digest.

"The power of life and death over others? Are you sure that this was written by someone who is sane and sensible?"

"Yes Ken. My research had gone beyond the usual karate manual theory that most people were doing. That is why Malcolm was unhappy with me when I gave my talk. He must have thought I chickened out and to be honest I did."

"It will certainly account for your anxiety about giving that speech. But put me out of my misery will you. Who wrote the piece and what was it about?"

Leon took about a deep breath before answering, "The piece was written by the Dalai Lama and the subject was the Bubishi and the technique called the *dim mak*."

Ken gasped, "Poison hand!"

"Yes, He wrote that the Bubishi holds the secret to using the delayed death touch."

Chapter 13

The bustling city of Shanghai was complete chaos for the group as they made their way from the port after an unusually long journey. Street sellers where trying to attract people's attention to the food that was on display as they moved past them. Children ran around playing and getting in everybody's way while other people went in and out of buildings conducting unseen business, seeing friends or other such activities. Jano led the way through this neighbourhood while the rest of them looked around with both suspicion and interest. Chojiro noted that Jano knew exactly where to go and asked him why.

"I came here several years ago with Takahara San when we attempted to find the founder, Master Ku Sanku."

"Did you find him, Jano?"

"No, we did not. We did however find some relatives of his."

Chojiro raised an eyebrow.

"A daughter, the man she married plus a son. For all intents and purposes, we are heading back to the spiritual home of our brotherhood."

"I thought that was the temple in Henan province?"

"Ah yes, the temple to Daruma is the home of our spiritual leader, but the brotherhood was founded in the home of the man who led us on our paths to him. This will also become home for your wife and unborn child while we go on our journey of honour."

Chojiro thought about what Jano had said for a second before saying, "Journey of honour? That's an interesting phrase you used there."

"I am merely quoting a reference about a prophecy of returning the Bubishi to its home that Master Ku Sanku described as the Journey of Honour. He said only four would go on this journey. We are fulfilling that part of his prophecy as we speak."

"I never knew that the Master could predict the future?"

"If you'd had time to finish your studies, you would have discovered a lot of things about our Master."

"Do we have far to go?" said Chojiro changing the subject.

"It is just round this corner," answered Jano. He led the way while Chojiro and the rest of the group followed him.

The sight that greeted him could not have surprised Chojiro more. If this was the birthplace of a brotherhood that was destined to hold a document of such magnitude as the Bubishi, you would never have known. This house was very much in keeping with the style of the neighbourhood. It was rickety, ramshackle and dirty while there was steam coming from behind it as though someone was cooking. Jano was heading towards the door, while the rest of the group hung back and waited. As he came near it, he found a thin rope hanging from above and he pulled. It emitted a high ringing sound from a bell that Chojiro could not see and it summoned a person who proceeded to have a hushed conversation with Jano. When he gestured for them to move towards the house, Chojiro led the way followed by Shumi, while Gogen and Kosaku brought up the rear. They all entered the house each bowing to the woman who had been gracious enough to allow them in. Gogen was thankful the most. He had looked up at the skies to see the weather looking as though it was taking a turn for the worse and was quite glad he had not decided to stay on the boat. It would have been a rough ride home. They made themselves as comfortable as they could in a room as small as this and waited for Jano to make the introductions as they looked at the two other people who were already in the room when they arrived.

"May I introduce the daughter of our master Suki Chang. The man to your left is her husband Li and the other to the right is their son Mao." Each of the Chang's took a bow as Jano said their names and after a slight uncomfortable pause Suki announced, "I'll make some tea while you men talk. Come Shumi. Will you help me?"

Shumi nodded and followed Suki out of the room.

Jano started the conversation, "It is good to see you again, Li. I see you are well."

"Yes Jano, we are well. But tell me old friend, what brings you to our house?"

"Are you aware that Chojiro's wife is pregnant?"

"No I am not. Surely your visit to Shanghai is more than just for the medical attention?"

"We are on the journey of honour."

Li rose on eyebrow and did the maths, "Five become four. Very good Jano, you are reading the signs and I see you have also done your research."

"You know how much I have studied his book."

"Yes, that book should be well read. Even my son, Mao, has read it. I would consider it essential reading for anyone on the path my father-in-law set for his students."

Kosaku interrupted this potential argument, "What book are you talking about?"

This time Mao answered, "The book of predictions. It is written by Master Ku Sanku. Only those who have earned the right can read it. You have to prove that you are ready. My grandfather said those of us who read the predictions too early could do damage rather than good."

"Why don't you tell the rest of my group the prediction that myself and your father are talking about, Mao?" asked Jano.

"Very well. The prediction that you are referring to is known as The Journey of Honour. My grandfather said that at the time the brotherhood is at its most vulnerable, our enemy will take away the protector leaving the gifted one with the ancient and most noble text. The gifted one will select four others who will help him to take our text back to its rightful home where the enemy cannot get to it. However, on the journey one will not go any further meaning the five become four."

"Excellent, Mao. Your knowledge is good, you have been taught well."

"Thank you, Jano," replied Li, "he is an excellent student. I have known for some time that he is capable of reading the predictions and being able to deal with them."

"Sorry, excuse me," interrupted Gogen who had been listening intently to this conversation and now really felt the need to ask a question that had been bothering him for some time, "this whole journey has been planned for a long time?"

"Not exactly planned, more like expected." explained Jano.

"Now I know why you asked me to join you."

"Please forgive my deception, Gogen," Jano said as he inclined his head towards him.

The conversation began in earnest as the group plus Li and Mao discussed what should be done next. Various statements ranging from staying where they are to finding maps for the journey where offered for debate and argument. Meanwhile, in the kitchen the two women where having a discussion of their own...

"How are you taking the news?" asked Suki.

"I'm fine if a little shocked. Chojiro is over the moon but I'm not sure what's going to happen."

"What do you mean?"

"This journey of honour."

"There is no doubt it is dangerous, Shumi."

"What if he doesn't come back?"

"You need to have a little faith. Li and Mao are unconcerned about the details of the journey, only that it has been undertaken and the reasons why. My father predicted these events but did not plan the entire journey, so everybody is having to use their own interpretations to what my father wrote and learn as they go along."

"I know but I would not be a good wife if I did not worry about him."

"You are a good wife!" giggled Suki, "come, lets take this tea to the men." They both picked up trays in front of them and made their way out of the kitchen and into the main room of the house where they laid them down on the table the men where sitting around before retreating into the corner of the room allowing them to debate, argue and drink until it was very late and everybody had grown tired. As everybody was getting relaxed and ready to sleep, Jano turned to

Suki and said, "You do realise we could be away for quite a while?"

"Yes, Jano."

"We might not come back at all."

"I know my role in this Jano. I too have read the prophecy my father made about this journey and I am prepared to wait a long time."

"Good," replied Jano, " because the mood Chojiro is in at the moment, we could be moving very slowly tomorrow."

"How do you mean?"

"Have you noticed he hasn't said a word since Mao explained the journey to us?"

* * * * * * * * * * * *

Chojiro was so deep in thought that he only had a couple of drinks by the time everybody started to drift off to sleep. When Mao had started to explain the journey to everyone Chojiro knew and understood straight away what a long distant memory of a conversation with Takahara was beginning to mean. He thought it had long since left the memory but it continued to lurk at the edges of his mind, waiting for the moment it would be needed and now the time had arrived. Chojiro didn't want to relive it as it brought back memories of such a cherished time with someone who was important and influential in his life but the scene began to replay in his mind. He could see it as if it was only yesterday.

"Yes Sensei, you wish to see me?" asked Chojiro.

"I do, Chojiro. Have I never told you how good your studies are at the moment," said Takahara

"All the time Sensei," blushed Chojiro. He never could take compliments gracefully.

"Do I? My memory is not as good as it once was. Its not important," Takahara waved away the comment before changing the subject, "Chojiro, I need you to promise me that no matter how special you become you will always keep your feet on the ground." Takahara made this statement with a forceful look in his eyes that Chojiro will never forget.

"Why do I need to promise you that?" Chojiro replied.

"You will know why when it happens."

Chojiro shook his head at such a daft request, "I'm not that special. Nor will I ever be."

"Promise me."

Chojiro shook his head again. He was not happy to promise something he knew would not happen.

"Please. Promise me."

It was the fact that Takahara had used the word please, which made Chojiro take notice as he had never heard him say the word before. It was not what was expected of a teacher/pupil relationship. He looked at Takahara for a long time before saying, "If it means that much then yes, I promise." Takahara visibly relaxed.

"But now you will have to explain to me why I would become so big headed and self important."

"All in good time, Chojiro."

Takahara never told him what it was all about. Yet Chojiro still kept the promise he made, as anything else would be disrespectful, but made a mental note for tomorrow to ask Jano why he was never told about all this. He turned away from everyone and laid down in the corner of the room. He propped his head up on his forearm and slowly fell asleep not realising he was the last one to do so.

Chapter 14

Ken sat back in his seat of the taxi and let out a long slow breath while Leon watched expectantly. Their brief silence was punctuated with darting glances at the taxi driver who was too busy humming a tune from the last Bollywood film he had been watching to realise there was a tense situation developing in his car. He followed behind a large MPV which he decided didn't suit the blackened windows.

"Come on Ken, say something," as Leon watched him.

"I don't know what to say," replied Ken, "this isn't some Hollywood fantasy or mythical novel you know."

"Yes Ken. Don't believe for one second that I have found this easy to deal with," said Leon, "the whole thing has started since the Dalai Lama posted his blog, two days ago. I don't think for one second its a coincidence."

"It just sounds so far-fetched."

"I know, lets get back to mine and we'll discuss this further. I'll even show you the posting on the website."

The taxi continued to make its way along Manchester Road following the MPV when all of a sudden the taxi driver had to break suddenly. The MPV had screeched to a halt. The driver let rip with a volley of abuse when a familiar oriental man got out holding a gun. He lifted his arm, took aim and squeezed the trigger. The taxi driver reeled twice as each bullet hit him before remaining silent and still. Ken and Leon made for the doors of the taxi but in true fashion of the cabs, the driver had locked the doors so as to prevent them getting out of the taxi and not paying the fare. They were trapped. The man walked to the front door of the car, opened it dragging out the now deceased taxi driver and got in. The gun was constantly trained on the pair of them as the man stated, "The Bubishi, please."

Leon replied, "Its in the file."

"Pass it to me."

Leon slowly turned to his right, picked up the file and handed it to the man. He opened the file and checked the contents. He was pleased to see a collection of papers with the front page written in an archaic but nonetheless recognisable form of Chinese confirming it was indeed the Bubishi.

"Thank you, gentleman."

The man exited the vehicle and placed something under the wheel arch before continuing towards the car in front.

Leon took one look and said to Ken, " We need to get out!"

"What? While he is still nearby?"

"Yes!"

Leon leant forward frantically pressing every button he could find as the MPV spun round and began to move away from the taxi. The exit doors remained shut until he pressed one button and heard the locks unclick. Ken slid the door aside and the pair of them bolted for the nearest wall as the oriental man fished for a remote device on his passenger seat and pressed the button on it.

The taxi exploded into a ball of flames.

* * * * * * * * * * * * *

The first time Victor and Susan realised that this explosion on Manchester Road involved Leon and Ken was when they responded to the call of an incident and arrived at the scene. They found Leon and Ken propped against a wall talking to some firemen about what happened.

"Just when I thought I was not going to see you for a while, there is an incident less than twenty minutes later and you're involved," said Victor, with a smile on his face.

Susan signalled to the firemen to leave them alone.

Looking a little sheepish, Leon replied, "It was him again."

"Mister Chinese Porsche? How did he know where to find you?"

Leon paused realising he had an opportunity to go back from what he was about to say, but the moment had gone. Victor stood there hands on hips, looking at him expecting an answer.

"I think there might be someone feeding information to him on the inside of your police station," stated Leon.

Victor had been ready for this and immediately shot back a reply, "How do you know?"

"This," he presented the badge he had grabbed during his fight in the Carrera to Victor.

"Its just a badge."

"A badge I found belonging to the man who did this."

Victor thought about what Leon was saying. The idea that there was someone inside his own police station feeding information and, by the evidence before him, access to sources of equipment and explosives too, was maddening. Not all of it made sense and the only evidence he had was Leon's word, but he now realised there was no way back from this.

He forced out a breath to calm him, before asking, "What did he want?"

"Something given to me," replied Leon with a look on his face that Victor caught.

"Did they get it?"

Leon shook his head and patted his jacket where the inside pocket was located, "just the diary notes and the excerpt."

"I've got the rest of the diary, though," interjected Ken.

"And we are not going back to the police station," said Leon, "not until this problem is sorted."

"I understand, but why didn't you say something in the interview room?" asked Victor.

"You wouldn't have believed me," Leon stated.

"I still don't believe you now."

"Then this was just a road rage incident?" Leon never took his gaze off Victor.

Susan noted the rage in his eyes. They were a force to be reckoned with and now she was beginning to understand why Leon was a successful at what he did. When she first met him she thought that he was meek, possibly even mild. Now she was re-thinking her opinion of him and realised that perhaps Leon was a far stronger person, which gave her an idea. She wasn't sure whether anybody would like it, but it would suit their purposes exactly.

"Why don't we see if Leon would be prepared to help catch this oriental man?" she offered.

All three men turned to her, before Leon said, "How?"

"We say we are bringing Leon into protective custody. All we have to do is let Leon's location be openly known as if we don't even think that there is someone on the inside. This will show whether we have a mole inside and will help us apprehend this man."

Victor thought about this, "I don't know, Susan. This is a little risky. Do you think Hadrian will go for this?"

Leon interrupted, "He will if I am willing to do it."

"I'm not sure about this. Having Leon as bait leaves a whole number of potential problems here, Susan," said Victor.

"We're doing nothing more than we would be doing at this point anyway. You know the procedure for something like this," answered Susan, "all we are going to do is keep a closer, more personal eye on Leon, that's all."

"I want to do it," Leon said, "I want to find an end to all this."

"I suggest we talk to Hadrian about this first," stated Victor as he made his way back to the car, "which means you are going to have to come back to the police station."

Susan looked at Leon and nodded to him. If they could convince their superior this was a good idea, things can start to happen. All it needs is a few well placed calls and conversations and the plan would be in motion. As Susan followed Victor some way behind to the car, she fished in her bag to find her mobile. She opened it, pressed a button on the speed dial and waited for it to answer. She was talking intently into it as she got into the car.

Leon turned to Ken, who was wearing a worried expression. For everything he had done in his life, he realised for the first time that there are consequences to his actions. More importantly, those consequences affected someone sat at home carrying his child.

"Are you sure about this?" enquired Ken.

"We need to force the issue on this. I can't see any other way."

"What are you going to do if this goes wrong?"

"I'll deal with it then."

"How?"

"I don't know, Ken. I really don't want to think about it, to be honest."

The black Astra pulled up in front of them driven by Victor with Susan in the front passenger seat. Victor's expression was clearly showing that he was uncomfortable with Susan's idea and was working through every scenario that could happen so as to find reasons not to run with this plan. Susan just looked stony-faced. Both of them didn't even look at Ken and Leon as they got in the car. The black Astra did a u-turn in the road and headed back to the police station.

* * * * * * * * * * * *

Victor's voice could be clearly heard booming down the corridor coming from Hadrian's office as

Leon and Ken sat on some plastic chairs a little way further down from the door. It was obvious from the tone of voice that Victor was remonstrating quite forcefully with Hadrian about this idea and when there was a quieter voice talking, it was followed by Victor's voice coming back at it even louder and forceful than before. After listening to this go on for about twenty minutes, the door shot open and Victor stuck his head round.

"Do you want to come in?" he said grumpily, still clearly unhappy with the turn of events in the office.

Leon and Ken filed into the office to be greeted by Hadrian and Susan. John Hadrian was a small, thin man wearing glasses. He was wearing a short-sleeved white shirt which was immaculately pressed and a perfectly knotted navy blue tie. His office was clean and tidy with a plant pot in the corner of the room and the desk was facing away from the window which had a view of the main road outside the station and a backdrop of the town centre of Huddersfield with the hills of the Yorkshire dales in the background. Hadrian looked at Leon intently. His forehead was creased with lines and his grey hair was receding at a rate that was quite astonishing. In fact, Leon noted that he reminded him of a former England football manager and suppressed a small smile as he was invited to sit at a chair next to a bank of filing cabinets. Victor continued to stand with his arms folded while Ken stood next to him. Susan, rather strangely, stood behind Hadrian.

"You are aware of the dangers of this plan?" began Hadrian.

"Yes," replied Leon.

"You realise there is to be no playing the hero?" continued Hadrian.

"Yes."

"The minute you see or hear anything, you move away and stay where you are told to?"

"I will."

"There will be armed officers waiting to take over the minute this man enters the scene, it is important that you move out of the way."

"Don't worry about that, I will let the professionals do their job," said Leon.

"That's good, because I don't need to tell you that Victor here is not exactly happy with this entire plan."

"Neither am I," interrupted Ken, "people like us are not meant to be involved in things like this."

"I understand," said Hadrian, turning to face Ken, "but I think the unusual circumstances regarding this case call for unusual solutions."

Susan continued, "We have a unique opportunity to catch this man before he starts to wreak havoc as he becomes more desperate to get to Leon."

"But it doesn't mean that we should use his actual target as bait," began Victor.

"And so the argument goes round and round," Hadrian said, stopping the voices in the room, "we have been through this all before. I understand all sides of the argument, even sympathise with you, Victor, but we have to do something and I believe this is the best opportunity while keeping the risk as low as possible."

Victor shook his head.

"The decision has been made. You know the plan, I suggest we start to put it into place," continued Hadrian, "good luck Leon, follow the procedures and I will see you in a couple of hours."

"Thank you," replied Leon.

They all started to file out of the room leaving Hadrian still at his desk. Leon's last look of him as he left the room was of him picking up the phone. As he did so he gave Leon a fleeting look and a nod. The only thing he could mean was one of encouragement. Leon returned the nod and carried on out of the office. Victor led Leon and Ken to the left, while Susan went right.

"Where is she going?" asked Ken.

"She's gone to organise and brief the armed squad we have waiting downstairs," Victor said as he looked after her and watched her put her mobile to her ear.

After everything that had happened, Leon realised he had not had time to put the Bubishi boxes in a safe place. Now was the time to do something about it. He turned to Victor and asked whether he could have some privacy before all this started.

"Sure, follow me," answered Victor.

He led them down a corridor and opened the door at the end. Leon and Ken followed. As the door was shut behind them Leon began.

"We need to put this somewhere safe," he said, taking the Bubishi boxes out of his inside pocket.

"I can put them in the safe at the academy," said Ken.

"Too obvious and we don't have the time," said Leon, with a shake of his head. He turned to look at Victor.

"What about my locker here at the police station?" Victor offered.

Leon thought for a moment. Leaving it in this police station where there could be someone out to get the Bubishi sounded ridiculous, bordering on dangerous, yet it was because of those very reasons he thought that it might actually be a good idea.

"Can we do it without anybody else knowing?" he asked.

"Sure, the locker room is just around the corner from here."

"Let's go."

They made their way out and headed straight for the locker room. Taking care to make sure that no one could see them, Victor punched in the security code on the keypad next to the door and the three of them moved into the room. They made their way to the back of the room where Victor brought out his bunch of keys, located the one for his locker before inserting and twisting. Inside was a collection of photos of a young girl with what looked like her mum and a pile of clothes. Leon placed the boxes into the locker and then closed the door checking to make sure it was locked. They went back to exit the room. Victor went first to check the corridor was clear before he motioned for Ken and Leon to come out also. By the time they got to door to go out of the police station and to the black Astra, no one would have guessed at what they had just done.

Susan was waiting at the car when the three men got there which Victor thought was quick for the briefing. When he asked her why she was here, she replied that Hadrian had called her and said he would brief the armed police and that she should go back and assist with the preparing of Leon and supervision of the protection around him. With a disgruntled look, Victor got in the car and the others followed suit.

As they were driving along, Leon noticed that the houses were getting smaller and shabbier as they continued along the road they were on which didn't bode well as far as he was concerned. There was people in hooded tops standing on street corners watching the car as it drove past looking mutinous at it as though they were intruding on their patch, while others greeted people walking up to them before small packages where exchanged. Drugs, thought Leon. He was about to ask Victor and Susan why they didn't do anything about it when the black Astra turned a corner and came into a cul-de-sac. At the end was a surprisingly well kept house with another black Astra waiting in the drive way.

They got out the car and entered the house. Inside it looked like an everyday house. Pans were arranged neatly on shelves, the cupboards were full of food and the washing machine was on and clothes were turning in the drum. In the living room, the only concession that this house was used by the police was the two uniformed constables sat down as they entered the room. Victor nodded his acknowledgement as he saw them, then turned to Leon.

"These two constables are here for your protection. They are under orders to contact us the minute they suspect our man is nearby. When they do, you are to do everything they say without exception. Me and Susan are going to be nearby and will move in when we get the call. Ok?"

Leon nodded. Victor and Susan left the room.

"What do we do now?" asked Ken.

"Wait for something to happen I suppose," replied Leon.

Ken, who is not noted for his patience, started to pace the living room floor, stopping periodically to examine something on a shelf or the mantelpiece, while Leon sat down and just stared into space which got him thinking. How on earth is this connected with the dim mak. If you wanted to kill someone just use a gun or a knife. Unless you needed to leave no evidence. An assassination then? But who would you practice on? The last thought chilled Leon to the bone. He really did not want to think about that one. He understood the theory that to cause someone to die after a period of time and not immediately, you needed to hit someone in a particular place at a particular time of day in a particular way, but to actually use it practically after all these years was a very disconcerting thing....

BANG!! Leon was disturbed from his thoughts by the sound of gun shot coming from the kitchen. Ken was also turning towards the kitchen when one police officer came hurtling through the door. He had time to shout, "Run!!" before another gun shot came from the kitchen which caught the officer in the back before he fell to the floor. Ken heeding his advice ran out the patio windows at the back of the living room into the garden before vaulting over the fence.

Leon meanwhile was hemmed in by the shot police officer and the person advancing towards him with a gun. He looked wide-eyed in shock as the person walked calmly towards him before shutting the kitchen door.

"I don't understand!" Leon exclaimed.

"You don't need to," replied Susan, "now, I suggest if you want to continue to live, you should do as I say and go to the garage."

Leon did as he was told and went to the garage followed by Susan, who never moved her gun away from Leon. As he went through the door he saw a white car which started up the moment he arrived. Susan lifted the boot lid and intimated for Leon to get in. When he had done so, Susan opened the doors to the garage and as the car moved out, she quickly closed them shut again. The white car calmly drove off and turned the corner while Susan got out her radio and putting on her best distressed voice called, "Quick! Everybody scramble! Subject ambushed! Two officers down!"

She then took a rock from one of the garden beds and a small knife from her handbag. She dropped the stone on the floor in front of her and then proceeded to cut herself above the eyebrow. She grimaced in pain while she did it before she slumped against the wall of the house next to the driveway.

Victor heard the call over the radio, two minutes after Susan said she was just going to run through some last minute procedure changes with the Police Constables. She had told him that she would take their car and join him when she had finished briefing them.

"Go!!!" shouted Victor into his radio before he gunned the engine of the black Astra and sped off ahead of everyone else. He arrived at the safe house to find Susan, bleeding from a head wound, slumped against the house with Ken tending to her in the driveway. As he ran up to them, he checked Susan to make sure she was Ok before going into the house and surveying the scene. He shook has head sadly before going back outside. *How many people are going to die for this Bubishi?'* thought Victor as he moved towards the advancing police officers and started to supervise the investigation looking at how exactly someone had got to Leon so easily.

Chapter 15

In his private chambers, Lord Shimazu was in talks with his personal samurai about the way to proceed.

"I think I should be going over there myself!" he stated.

"My lord, I think you should exercise some prudence," replied his confidante.

"This whole exercise has been badly organised and carried out from the start. The venture could use my resourcefulness," asserted Shimazu.

"That maybe so," began the samurai, "but you are needed here. If the emperor were to come, how would we explain why you are not here?"

Shimazu thought for a second before murmuring, "True," and nodded.

The samurai pressed his advantage, "Your friend is as resourceful as yourself. They will deliver what you desire. Once you have that, you will have the power of life and death itself."

"Very well, Minamoto, I will stay here…"

"My lord!" A man hurried into the room and bowed deeply. He was holding what looked like a letter, "I have a message for you from China."

Shimazu took the letter from the messenger, dismissing him with a wave of his hand and began to read. After a while a smile sprung from his face.

"You are indeed a wise man, Minamoto."

"I am?" he replied.

"Yes! My friend has the Bubishi within their grasp. They should have it in the next few days."

* * * * * * * * * * * *

All was quiet in the Chang house during the night when all of a sudden a figure dressed in black and was hooded entered the house from the rear. It would stop occasionally at the slight snuffle or snort of some of the occupants but once they had died down, the figure would start to move again. Eventually they got into the living room and found Chojiro. They slowly and silently crept over to him. The figure surveyed him for signs of the legendary boxes upon his person. Things were difficult because of the lack of light, but surely that bulge over the left side of his chest was what they were looking for? Slowly they crouched down by Chojiro's side and reached out their hand and started to insert it into his robes. All of a sudden, Chojiro stirred and turned away from the figure, trapping their hand under his armpit. This was not what they had expected and had to think quickly by gently lifting the arm and retrieving it. In the background light was starting to filter through, signalling the break of dawn and the silent figure knew time was passing. They needed to get the boxes and quickly. Sweat was beginning to develop on their forehead. Time for drastic action was needed. They went straight for the boxes as quickly as they could and Chojiro was immediately awoken by the roughness of this move. He looked up to see someone stood over him grasping at the place where the Bubishi boxes were. He grabbed the hand and twisted, while pressing his thumb into the inside of the hand by the fleshy part and dug his first two fingers just below the first knuckle. This caused the figure to recoil and cry in pain. Sensing the weakness, Chojiro stood up and brought his feet over and fell back to the floor, locking the arm he was holding and then lifting his hips. He held the position just before the point he could break the arm and dislocate the shoulder.

In pain, the figure cried, "Please stop! Please!"

Jano, who heard the commotion and had run to help Chojiro, was stood over the pair of them, "Let go, Chojiro. This person isn't going anywhere now."

Chojiro relented upon hearing Jano's voice and got up, never taking his gaze away from the prone figure. Jano walked over to this masked figure and removed their hood.

Li, who had joined everyone in the main room, looked astonished as he quickly realised that the person who had had their hood removed was in fact his son, Mao.

"Why?!" he exclaimed.

"I want to see the Bubishi!" returned Mao.

"Then why didn't you ask?"

"Because the things I wanted to see are not even known to *him*," Mao cocked his head in Chojiro's direction.

"He is the gifted one. He is not to know what is in it until he is ready," said Li.

"I know but it doesn't stop me seeing what it is," said Mao with an insolent look on his face.

Jano had been watching this conversation when a wave of comprehension came over him, "*Dim mak*," he whispered to himself.

"I'm sorry," replied Li, "did you just mention the poison hand?"

"Chojiro, Kosaku, Gogen please get your things. Shumi, you will be safe here when we are upon our journey. Until then, please go back to Suki."

The three men made their way to their possessions picking up various little things as they went, while Shumi returned to an unseen part of the house.

"What is going on here?" demanded Li, looking around bewildered.

"I'm sorry my friend, we must go. The Bubishi is not safe." Jano returned.

"Why? I know Mao has stepped out of line, but only through curiosity."

"No, something you said has made me realise we need to go. It is said that only those ready to handle what is said in the book of predictions can study it. I put it to you that your son is doing more damage than good."

"Jano, I...."

Without a word of warning, Mao lunged at Chojiro with a guttural shout. Li moved toward them and pulled away his son while Kosaku and Gogen came to Chojiro's aid.

Li turned to Jano while still holding back his struggling son, "Jano, you misunderstand me..."

Jano cut in, "There is no misunderstanding. The Bubishi is unsafe in the presence of your son!"

With that, Jano, Chojiro, Gogen and Kosaku left the house.

"Jano!" Shouted Li. The group ignored him and didn't look back. He walked to the door at the front overlooking the street and watched on as they turned the corner and a wave of sadness came over him as he did not the get chance to say it wasn't him who showed Li the book of predictions. He turned to look at his son who had now crumpled to the floor and was sobbing gently. He helped him to stand up before walking back into the house.

* * * * * * * * * * * *

"I don't understand, Jano, why did we have to leave the house so quickly and without breakfast may I add?" asked Gogen as they continued to walk through the streets of Shanghai.

"Because Mao knew something about the Bubishi that he should not have done. He was not ready for such knowledge. Now you see how true Master Ku Sanku's thoughts and teachings in the book of predictions are," replied Jano.

"Sure, but what was so dangerous that he wanted to know?" Gogen continued.

Jano stopped walking and looked at the group around him and another of his masters predictions came into his head. *'The cycle continues..'*

Instantly, Jano understood he was the last one with the knowledge and that the people before him where the key to it all starting again and helping to keep the book and hence its knowledge safe. He now knew exactly how Master Ku Sanku must have felt as he was about to impart the secret to his select few, including Takahara, all those years ago.

"I think its time we found somewhere to eat," he stated.

"Good, I'm starving!" returned Gogen

"Yes, we must not journey on an empty stomach," agreed Kosaku.

It was only Chojiro who noted that Jano wanted to talk as well and wondered exactly what it was he wanted to tell them all, "Does it have something to do with the Bubishi?"

"Nothing gets past the gifted one, does it?" smiled Jano.

They continued along the road until they found a place that sold rice cheaply enough and sat down to eat.

Before anyone could say anything Jano began, "As we sit here, we are the remaining members of the brotherhood of Ku Sanku. We sit here as one eating this rice and yet only I know the true secret that the Bubishi holds. So it is in my best interests that I tell you all because if I don't and something happens to me on this journey, the secret dies with me. To all of you here the Bubishi represents a manual that you work from to practice moves, techniques and strategies against an opponent and for the main part that is as far as most peoples knowledge goes. However there is a section that shows you how to perform a technique which if you strike at the right part of the body at the correct time you can cause certain death, not immediate death, but certainly the person will die. Maybe in an hour, a day, maybe a week, even two years. But nonetheless, they will die of the injury sustained from the move. This technique is known as Dim Mak. The effect is as though someone has been poisoned; therefore we know it as poison hand. That is what caused me to leave the Chang house earlier than expected. Mao knew about this and wanted to see it for himself. I don't want to know what he was going to do with the knowledge he would have gained but I think it would be to no good use. He was not ready and would have become everything that

Master Ku Sanku said. This is the reason why our dojo was raided by the Satsuma and this is why we are here travelling to Henan province. We cannot let the secrets of the Bubishi fall into the wrong hands. I realise that I was the last person to know all this but now with your help, my friends, we will lead our book to its destined safe place and then we can relax and carry on with our lives and studies."

"Hold on," began Gogen, "all this travelling is about a move that can kill someone?"

"Not just a killing move, but it is about the power of life and death. Just imagine what you could do if you held the secret to this move. You could assassinate without anybody finding out. Perform the move on someone and hold them to bribery or ransom. You could use it as a drawn out, vindictive death penalty for criminals or enemies. The reason isn't the move itself, it's the hold over people it will gain you. How would you feel if you knew your leaders have the power to decide when you live and when, or how, you die? It could be everybody we know, love and live with. Whole countries would live in fear and it's this fear which could be used by the Satsuma to continue their stranglehold over all of Okinawa."

"Why do we hold the secret to this move?" Kosaku asked.

"Because we are the one group of people who would never use the move for personal gain. We would only use it in a last gasp, life or death moment. That is why our brotherhood guards this secret because we are well equipped to deal with the issues surrounding the use of this move. Do you not understand why there is such a great deal of emphasis placed on your religious studies now? As Buddhists we are brought up to respect all forms of life and this allows us to reflect on the monumental charge that has been given to us."

They continued the rest of the meal in silence before they got up from the table they were sitting at and made their way back onto the street. Chojiro had sat and listened intently to what Jano had to say while eating and thought for a while longer.

"Do you really believe that we will be able to relax and lead normal lives again after this?" he eventually asked.

Jano looked at Chojiro and pressed his lips together. When the other two weren't looking he sadly shook his head before turning away from his questioner and leading the group on the road out of Shanghai.

Chapter 16

'Its not as comfortable as the Porsche' thought the driver, 'but it suits our purposes.'

To anybody walking through the streets of a down-ridden council estate in Huddersfield, to see the white car driving past would be nothing out of the ordinary. If you looked in the boot though, you would find something extraordinary.

As he drove along in the car, he continued to ponder, 'This man holds the one thing my family has craved for generations. To hold the secret that tells of the ultimate power over people has been something we have striven for as long as there has been a family.'

The *Kyokuryu-kai* of Okinawa was the local Yakuza to the area. Their office is still based in Naha and was what the man referred to as his family. In fact, he had been in touch with them only yesterday to report to his *Oyabun* how his mission to retrieve the Bubishi and bring it back to Okinawa, had been going.

"Your plan is nearing fruition?" said a voice at the other end of the phone.

"Yes sir."

"Good. I have people over here in Okinawa who are willing to pay handsomely for this document. The funds you requested for the police officer were received?"

"Yes, she has assured me she will perform her role perfectly. I will then forward her the extra money for providing us this opportunity."

"It was her idea and we reward our employee's who show commitment and ingenuity. Please pass on my thanks to her. It is well known that women and our family don't always work well together. However, in this case I will have to rethink."

"I will to see to it, sir"

"One last thing, Jirocho," the use of his name by his *Oyabun* made his back stiffen, "you have followed this document for us since you joined all those years ago. You know the price of failure. I hope I do not have to suffer the dishonour of you presenting me with something."

"I've not failed you yet," replied Jirocho.

"I know," replied the *Oyabun* before replacing the receiver on his phone cutting the line from Okinawa. Jirocho put his mobile phone down and nervously inspected his hands. He made a mental note as to which fingertip he would cut off if the worst happened before leaving his hotel room and making his way to the bar for a couple of beers to calm down with.

So the plan had come to fruition and he had Leon Rhodes in the boot of his car. He was now on his way to a building where Jirocho would find out where the Bubishi was. He had been assured by the police officer that this place would not be considered for inspection by the police and could guarantee a considerable time to interrogate Leon to know where the document was. Jirocho was convinced he would have it on his person and would therefore break quite easily. If his luck was in he would be out the country before the end of the day.

The building the car arrived at was some way out of the town. In fact, it was a dilapidated former farm building which had somehow escaped being demolished by the strange idea that it was a listed building. Jirocho parked in the field it was situated, got out then walked round to the back of the car and opened the boot.

Leon looked up and blinked wildly while his eyes got used to the sudden rush of light. He felt himself pulled roughly out of the car and led to a building. He didn't have time to see where he was as he was led too quickly and his eyes still hadn't got used to the light. All he could feel was something metal being pushed into his ribs and he quickly realised that it was a gun which meant that he had no chance of escape. Before long, he was led into the building the car had stopped next to and was pushed into a chair and tied to it. Leon took this time to get used to his setting. He saw he was in an open area with no internal walls and it was in a bad state of repair. The ceiling looked as if it was going to collapse at any given moment and there was a pile of plastic bags and empty beer cans in one corner from someone who had been here before. A dirty mattress was next to the rubbish and in the other corner was a concrete slab leant against the wall. Sunlight was peeking through the gaps in the windows which were catching the dust in the air making it look like there was many little flies buzzing around the building. Despite this unused feeling, Leon got the impression that this place was prepared for him when he looked to his left and saw a fold-up table and his abductor standing over it. Next to it was a blue cool box, similar to the one he used to put food in for picnics with Sarah when they first met. He seemed to be arranging something on the table before he turned to face Leon with a look of menace in his eyes. He knew this could be a long day and his thoughts continued on Sarah who had no idea what was now happening to him.

Jirocho walked towards Leon and surveyed him in his chair. There was a hint of heavy breathing which showed that he was nervous and the eyes looked a little wider than normal. 'Good', he thought, 'this should be over very soon.'

"Do you know why you are here?" Jirocho stated in his Japanese inflected English.

"Do you realise how many laws you have broken today?" replied Leon.

"Sure I do, I break many laws in many countries over many days. You see, its part of my life," returned Jirocho, "I, however, have the contacts and knowledge to make sure I always go home at the end of the day. Do you want to go home too?"

Leon stared back not saying a word.

"What? You don't want to go home?"

Leon shook his head. This was not making any sense to him whatsoever.

"What are you doing over here?" he asked.

Jirocho looked at him for a while, "You are not here to ask me questions. I am the one doing that."

"No, not you personally, all I'm interested in is why the Yakuza are here in Huddersfield?"

Jirocho reeled for a moment. He had not expected Leon to realise exactly what he was. The fact that he had not laid any clues made it that little bit more surprising. However, he was wearing the lapel pin which was in the shape and colour of his gang's emblem. Despite this, he recovered quickly.

"You are a perceptive man, Mr Rhodes," he said as he fingered the pin.

"I have lived my life being one."

It was this moment that Jirocho realised he was perhaps meeting someone who was not quite what he had originally seemed. Leon Rhodes was not the ordinary member of the public he had expected. He quickly decided to take this to next stage. He went back to the table and picked something up. He held it behind him and walked back towards Leon.

"Where is the Bubishi?" he demanded.

"I don't know what you are talking about," Leon quickly returned.

"I think you do. Where is the Bubishi?" Jirocho stated.

Leon simply said nothing and stared straight ahead.

Jirocho didn't react to Leon's silence. Instead his hand that he was holding behind him moved towards Leon's right hand which he had tied to the arm of the chair and pulled at the first finger. Leon was powerless to resist as Jirocho held the pruning secateurs he was hiding to his first finger at the first knuckle, just below his nail. Leon's breathing increased.

"You are aware of who I represent. Therefore you know the price of failure for us. Failure to tell me where the Bubishi is will result in you losing a fingertip much in the same way I would lose one for not giving my *Oyabun* the Bubishi. Every time I ask and you do not to tell me where it is, you pay the Yakuza price of failure."

Leon didn't say anything.

"Where is the Bubishi?"

Still Leon didn't reply. Jirocho increased the pressure of the blades against Leon's finger.

"I'll ask again. Where is the Bubishi?"

Leon looked fearfully at his finger before stating, "Whatever you do, please leave my wedding ring finger until last." He then burst out laughing.

"I promise," stated Jirocho.

With that he continued to increase the pressure on Leon's finger. With a last determined look at his captive he summoned all the strength he could muster in his hand and pressed his fingers together, causing the blades to slice through Leon's finger severing it at the knuckle joint.

All Leon could do was scream. The pain was just too much. With a last look at his captor the world turned black.

Jirocho looked at Leon feeling a slight wave of grudging admiration for him. It took no small amount of bravery to take that, particularly when you were not expecting it. He looked down at the hand with its mutilated digit and then bent over picking up the fingertip and placing it into a plastic bag which he had got from the table. He walked away from Leon and placed the bag into the cool box. He turned again to the table and picked up some gauze, bandages, cotton wool and disinfectant. The wound will need cleaning and dressing before it becomes infected or there will be another problem and Jirocho needed Leon alive long enough for him to find out where the Bubishi was. He set to work on his finger.

Leon woke and looked down at his right hand which now had a bandaged first finger. The tip of it was red from the bleeding and it stung like hell. He looked over to his captor who was smoking a cigarette and looking out of a gap in the boarded up windows.

"Expecting company are you?" he said to him.

Jirocho turned round, "Oh no, I'm not expecting anyone for a *long* time."

He walked back over to the table. Leon expected him to pick up the secateurs but was surprised to see Jirocho reach for the cool box lid, put his hand in and remove a clear plastic bag. In it was the severed fingertip. He showed it to Leon before replacing it with a smile.

"You can still save this you know. Just tell me where the Bubishi is and I'll let you take this and off you go," he mimicked the act of walking with his fingers.

"I know full well its not that easy," replied Leon.

"Look at your situation," countered Jirocho, "nobody knows you are here. There will be no rescue. You are quite alone and bound to that chair with no where to run and hide. Are you prepared to take the chance that you will not walk out of here?"

"There are more important things."

That's what, erm, Malcolm, I believe he was called, said before his head was removed."

"I thought you might have had something to do with it."

Jirocho laughed. Despite the seriousness of his job, this provided a little light entertainment. There really is something to be said for a little banter.

With lightening speed, Jirocho moved towards Leon and stopped within inches of his face.

"Where is the Bubishi?"

"Time for another finger chopping already?" asked Leon light heartedly.

"Something a little more base this time."

Leon remained silent. Jirocho took two paces back.

"Where is the Bubishi?"

Leon shook his head. Before he had chance to finish, Jirocho had leapt forward and viciously kicked him in the head. The chair toppled over on to the floor leaving Leon seeing the ceiling through a haze of stars caused by the kick. Jirocho stood over him and placed his foot over Leon's throat and pushed down. Leon shouted and shouted until Jirocho stopped. Then he repeated again and Leon did the same sounding like he was choking and shouting at the same time. This sequence was repeated for at least another five minutes until Jirocho turned away angrily and made his way over to a corner of the building. Leon had stopped coughing long enough to see Jirocho push the concrete slab to the floor. He dragged it slowly next to Leon. He then lifted one end and moved it above Leon's chest.

"Where is the Bubishi?" he asked again.

If Leon tried to answer, Jirocho would never know because he dropped the slab onto Leon and then stepped onto the slab creating a terrible weight on Leon's chest. After 5 seconds he lifted the slab and repeated his question. Leon didn't answer. Jirocho repeated this five times and still Leon wouldn't answer. Jirocho decided a break was needed, so he got off the slab and moved it to one side.

He turned round to see his captive breathing heavily and looking straight at him. If Jirocho didn't know any better, there looked to be fire in his eyes. By now most people would have given up. To take this kind of physical torture would have killed most people by now, but Leon was up to the task. Perhaps a little change of tack was needed. A more mental approach would reap dividends here.

"How are you doing, Mr Rhodes?" he asked.

Leon still couldn't speak. He just sat there panting heavily. There was a pain in his ribs where he thought he might have cracked two of them when the concrete slab was dropped and blood was seeping into his eye from the kick. Leon had to admit that one more going over would be all he could take. He needed to think quickly if he was going to survive this.

"How is your wife?"

"My wife? Don't bring her into this!" Leon's voice somehow returned to him.

"Why? She's very pretty," Jirocho picked up a photo of her walking out of the corner shop from the table and ran his finger down it circling at her chest.

"Don't go any where near her!" Leon was now trying to get out of his bindings.

"When this is over I might pay her a visit. I'll maybe borrow a badge and give her the bad news that she has lost her husband. She might need a shoulder to cry on..."

"I promise I will kill you if you go anywhere near my house!"

"Your house, of course!" Jirocho said triumphantly, "It's at your house"

The thought had never occurred to him until now. Despite being very resilient and determined, Leon was not a complicated man. He would store it close to him without thinking that it would be safer somewhere unconnected. He was just a member of the public at the end of the day. He trusted in these games to bring the truth to the surface and he found it very rarely failed.

Leon, meanwhile, was playing a very different game. He had decided to call a bluff in the hope that this man would move him out of this building and into a setting where he could call some shots. Unfortunately, that meant involving Sarah. But his house was one setting he was comfortable in. He feigned a bad poker face in the hope he would take the bait.

"Get up."

He had.

Jirocho started to untie Leon. He helped him to stand and Leon winced from his ribs as he did so.

"You keep that hand out of sight. Do you hear me?"

Leon nodded then led the way to the car. When they got in, Leon told Jirocho the way to his house and looked out of the window pensively as he watched the world go by. A different world now after everything that had happened. Before long, they had arrived at his house. As Leon got out, he thought he had seen Sarah in the window from behind the blinds, but he wasn't sure. After everything that had happened these past few days, he knew the minute she saw Leon get out of a strange car with a strange man, she would do what he was hoping she would do. He had no chance to check and would therefore have to rely on hope.

They arrived at the front door and Leon took his keys from his pocket and turned the lock. The door chime rang as he walked into his living room and Leon took this as his cue. He walked over to his desk and started looking through the drawers looking for a copy of the manuscript for his book. Jirocho looked on wondering what he was doing.

"You want the Bubishi?" Jirocho nodded, "then let me find it."

Jirocho stepped back from the desk and watched Leon rummage through his drawers.

As Leon started to wonder if he was going to find it, he saw a plain A4 envelope which told him what was there. He took the envelope and looked up at his captor. The scene before him was one of the most surreal he had ever seen. Jirocho was looking at Leon with the most patient look on his face while Sarah was stood behind him with a cricket bat in her hand about to hit him over the head. It was all Leon could do not to react. But he had and Jirocho turned round and looked at Sarah who was now nine months pregnant and snatched the bat from her.

"You ask your pregnant wife to do your dirty work?" he asked smiling benignly and continuing to look at Sarah, "no wonder you western men are becoming w....."

Jirocho never finished his sentence as Leon had hit him with a punch that started from way behind his hips. Jirocho lifted his hands and began to punch back but each time he did, Leon expertly blocked them. The feet where next to be used but Leon put distance between himself and Jirocho before coming back with kicks of his own. Jirocho reached for the lamp on his desk and swung at Leon who moved towards Jirocho and stopped him mid-swing then one, two, three knees to the stomach and he relinquished the lamp from Jirocho who looked at Leon holding his ribs and composed himself. He moved forward again bringing the chair of the desk with him and lifted it above his head. The movements where far too slow for Leon and he moved in and repeatedly punched his opponent. At this point Leon remembered the gun and moved forward to take it from Jirocho before he had time to pull it, but it was too late. Jirocho was now holding the gun in Leon's direction.

"Give me the Bubishi."

"You'll have to kill me first," replied Leon.

BANG!

Leon lurched in expectation of a bullet entering his body and the surge of pain he had already experienced today. However after fifteen seconds or so, he realised that no pain was coming to him at all. He opened his eyes and checked his body for a wound before looking up to see Jirocho unconscious on the floor and Sarah stood over him, breathing heavily and holding the poker from the fireplace. She had finally managed to hit him over the back of the head like they tried to do earlier without success.

Leon leant down and felt for the gun. When he had removed it, He looked around to see where the bullet had gone. There was a hole in the wall behind him and if the bullet had been mere centimetres closer, it would have hit Leon square in the face. Sarah noticed his bandages

"What's happened to your hand?"

Leon just cocked his head in Jirocho's direction, "I'll tell you later. You don't need to know right now."

"When I saw you coming with him, I knew something wasn't right."

"I know Sarah, I was banking on you doing what you did. It saved my life."

With that Leon picked up the desk chair and sat down at his desk. He reached in one of the draws and removed some insulating tape and handed it to Sarah. She began to tie up Jirocho while Leon reached for the phone and dialled.

* * * * * * * * * * * *

In the incident room of Huddersfield police station people were almost frantic with activity. Officers where sat in front of boards pinning up pictures of the safe house. Others were talking into phones. Yet more where in discussion with various officers before walking back to desks and typing furiously on computers.

At the centre of it all sat Victor and Susan who where constantly asked questions or given things to sign or giving orders. The phone in front of Victor began to ring and he picked it up just before Susan who had also made a grab for it.

"Detective Ugiagbe."

"Whatever you do, don't react. It's me, Leon."

To his credit, Victor didn't even flinch.

"Oh hi darling," Victor pressed his hand over the receiver and looked at Susan. He smiled, mouthed his wife's name and rolled his eyes while Susan returned the smile, "Yes dear?"

"Is Susan sat next to you?"

"Sure, sure. I'll pick some of that up for you."

"Susan sold the operation out. She's working for the Yakuza"

"All the way over there, dear. It's not exactly a short detour."

"Strange I know, but I'm the expert here. Meet me at my house. I'll contact Ken."

"Dinner ready at six? Ok, I'm nearly finished here anyway, Bye!"

Victor said his farewells explaining he had had enough for today and needed to get something for his wife for their tea. He walked out the incident room to jokes about being under the thumb and stopped off at the locker room to check that something was still in his locker before making his way to his car.

The conversation with Ken was far less coded.

"Ken, it's me, Leon."

"Thank god for that! What happened to you?"

"Oh the usual, kidnapping, finger chopping, crushed by concrete, the usual run of the mill day for me at the moment."

"You'll get over it, lad."

"Your sympathy is overwhelming, Ken. Anyway, get over here. Me, you and Victor need to talk."

"What? No Susan?"

"That's what we need to talk about. It's because of her I found myself in this."

"Right, on my way. What's that noise in the background?" Jirocho was trying to shout through his bindings but wasn't making any sense because the one on his mouth was muffling him quite well.

"You'll find out when you get here. See you soon."

Leon looked down at Jirocho and suddenly felt weak and tired. He realised his body had lost a lot of blood and had exerted himself to the extreme. To make matters worse, he felt cold.

'*Just shock,*' he thought as he grabbed his captive and dragged him into the kitchen to where Sarah was waiting with the gun they had removed from him.

"You know," he began grimly at Jirocho, "I could remove that fingertip for you now if you wish?"

Jirocho shouted an unmistakable "No!" even through the tape over his mouth.

Chapter 17

As the city of Shanghai gave way to the countryside, the debate amongst the group intensified as to how they were going to achieve their task.

"As long as no one comes across our path I reckon we could be there and finished within two weeks," said Gogen, hopefully.

Chojiro and Jano looked at each other.

"The only question I have is what we do when we get to the temple?" asked Kosaku.

"I've been thinking about that," started Chojiro as he turned to Jano, "what exactly do we do when we get the temple?"

"Whatever you see fit to do," replied Jano.

"You mean I could just hand it over and walk away?"

"Yes. I personally wouldn't recommend that though."

"What would you suggest I do then?"

"Oversee the preparations to keep it safe."

"You mean the monks are not expecting us?"

"They will be expecting us, they will only react once we have arrived."

"Well that's you and Jano occupied," said Gogen dryly, "but what about myself and Kosaku?"

Jano blinked at Gogen with his mouth slightly open. He hadn't considered the other two before now.

"We'll still need help with preparations for the Bubishi's safety. There will be something for everyone to do," appeased Chojiro.

Apparently satisfied, Gogen and Kosaku began talking to themselves as they continued on their path. The sun was beating down and the water in the rice fields shimmered causing the light to ripple slightly.

Changing the subject again, Chojiro asked Jano, "Perhaps we should tell them where we are going, my friend?"

The question had been expected and Jano heaved a sigh before stating, "I see we are no longer in Shanghai. I suppose I will tell them. Kosaku, Gogen. Come here please."

The other two turned round and listened intently.

"We are heading for Mount Song," Jano stated.

Kosaku laughed, "The sacred mountains? I knew we were heading for a temple in Henan, I just didn't realise we are going to *the* temple."

Gogen started to whimper slightly. This wasn't what he had wanted even if he secretly suspected it.

Chojiro, meanwhile, smiled appreciatively. It confirmed to him that the cause he was on now was just and true. This was something spiritual as well as physical and Chojiro was all the happier and contented with it. After initial misgivings about what he was doing, the closer they got to their destination the more he felt good about this journey.

Jano looked at the group again. All of them intently looked back at him and he had never felt more nervous. Things needed to be done and the closer they got to the temple the more difficult it was becoming to do it. Time was of the essence and they needed to be prepared when they arrived at the temple. He needed to spend some time alone with Chojiro to prepare him for the task he must fulfil. He looked up at the sky to see the sun was hanging low, just above the trees.

"I think we have travelled far enough for today. I say we find somewhere to camp and build a fire. Gogen, Kosaku, can I suggest that you look for some food for us all," and with that they all started to do their respective jobs. Jano and Chojiro started to build a fire while Gogen and Kosaku disappeared food hunting.

"I must talk to you, Chojiro," began Jano.

"What about?" came the reply.

"There is something in the book of predictions that you need to read," returned Jano.

"Does it concern me?" Chojiro asked.

"Yes it does. Here, let me find it for you."

With that, Jano started to rummage in his carry sack for a copy of his venerated master's book. Once he had found it, he opened the book and located the relevant section before handing it to Chojiro. He took it from Jano and began to read.

He glanced up from the book sometime later and said, "Are you sure about this?"

Jano nodded.

"Who exactly are we going to defend ourselves from?"

"I'm not certain. But my best guess will be one of two people. The first is the Chinese emperor while the second will be the Japanese one."

A rock and a hard place, thought Chojiro.

"However," continued Jano, "the Chinese will not allow the Japanese sovereign on their territory and he will not leave the country, so he might send a more appropriate representative with the Chinese in assistance to keep an eye on them. That will be the most likely case."

Chojiro turned away from Jano to think.

"I'm no general," he eventually said.

"I know, but the temple is defendable. You have to do this, you have to prove that you are worthy to hold the knowledge the book contains."

The warm feeling that had wrapped Chojiro only moments earlier had vanished and been replaced by an uncomfortable one. The thought of being responsible for the lives and in some cases, deaths, of a multitude of people did not sit right in his head.

They did not have a military class at the academy that could have prepared him for this.

"That is why I am here, Chojiro. Before I joined the brotherhood, I was a member of the Ryukyu army. I was never in command but I did study the theories behind modern warfare. We will be outnumbered but I feel we can make things difficult enough for them to even things a little. That is the best way for us to look at this."

Chojiro considered Jano's words. His friend was prepared to stand with him and help him make the decisions he didn't like but must make, nonetheless. The warm feeling he had lost only moments ago returned.

"Very well, Jano. A guess and a suggestion from you is a certainty and a decision made as far as I am concerned," a smile returned to Chojiro's face, "Let's get this fire started. Kosaku and Gogen will be back soon."

Nothing more was said until the other two returned. They had found a chicken roaming a field from a nearby farm. They had cornered it, eventually catching and strangling it. They brought it back with them and it was plucked and roasted before long. While they watched the bird roast, Chojiro informed them of the intended plan when they got to the temple. Gogen took the news stoically, while Kosaku happily carried on as though he hadn't been told, after which they continued to concentrate on the cooking meat, lost in their own thoughts. Chojiro decided not to carry on the debate about what they were going to do unless someone wanted to. The conversation stayed away from the future for the next few days and stayed firmly about wondering what was happening at home.

* * * * * * * * * * * *

The ship docked in Shanghai and it carried the insignia of someone who was representing the Emperor of Japan. A delegation of Chinese was waiting for them to disembark. Finally, Shimazu of Satsuma stepped off the ship, walked to the awaiting delegation and bowed deeply.

"I am here with humble thanks from the Emperor of Japan," he stated.

"You will travel with an appointed person of this country," began the leader of the group, "this is the person."

Another member of the group stepped forward.

"Begging your indulgence, but I know of someone who I would prefer to accompany us on our journey," offered Shimazu.

"Who is it?" asked the group leader.

"Their name is Chang and they live not far from here."

"Very well, they will be sent for."

One of the group turned and ran for their horse once Shimazu had provided the address and it was not long before he returned with a figure that was very familiar to Shimazu.

The group leader addressed the figure. "You are aware of the task that has been given you?"

"I am," was the reply.

"You are the emperor's representative for this group. You will make a decision, when needed, as though He was making it himself. We trust they will be the right ones."

The group then made their way from the docked ship allowing Shimazu to go to his appointed representative.

"How long has it been since they left your house?" he asked.

"Five days."

"We have much time to make up."

"How strong is your army?"

"I am only allowed one hundred soldiers on foot and fifty horse-mounted. The Chinese Emperor would allow no more for fear of an invading army."

"It will be enough, my Lord. There will be four brotherhood members and about fifty unarmed monks from the temple. Skilled fighters though they will be, we have the superior numbers and the men are armed."

"You are sure we have to do this?"

"Yes, it is foretold in the book of predictions."

"You are sure that we will get the Bubishi?"

"The relevant prediction says that the sacred book will be carried out of the temple by the victor of the battle. We are going to the temple with an army that will ensure victory, therefore we are fulfilling prophecy."

"Very well. We will move out once the ship is unloaded. I am, however, unhappy at being summoned here. I have pulled many a favour for you so I can do as *you* wish. I therefore will not tolerate failure," stated Shimazu.

"I would not have asked you here unless I thought victory was a certainty."

* * * * * * * * * * * *

By now the days had turned into weeks and Chojiro had been doing some thinking regarding the defence of the temple when they arrived. Some mountains had started to show themselves on the horizon and the group knew they were not far from where they needed to be.

Chojiro turned to Jano and said, "I think you should teach us how to do it."

"To do what?" he replied.

"*Dim Mak.*"

An uneasy silence overcame the two of them while Jano considered this statement.

"I think you're right," Jano eventually replied.

Chojiro said nothing more. He walked ahead to Gogen and Kosaku and was soon in deep conversation.

For a few more days while they travelled, Kosaku, Gogen and Chojiro could be seen practicing the moves until they were memorised. On the fifth day of practising, the land started to make an upward turn.

Jano turned to his pupils and said, "It is prophesised that our enemy will attack at a time that allows us the best opportunity to show our potency. I predict that our master is referring to the time of day they will attack and allow us to use this move. Because of how close we are to the temple, I have shown you the correct version only for the time I think it will happen."

The others nodded, except Chojiro. He remained in thought for a few more moments before a question began to form in his mind which he allowed to come to his lips.

"Why does the time of day have such importance?" he asked.

Jano motion for them to stop what they were doing and sit down with him by a big tree dominating the clearing they were practicing in.

Jano drew a rudimentary human form in the dirt in front of him with a stick he had found laid on the floor before speaking, "The human body has many points through which the life force, *Chi*, flows through it. The main points that we are interested in to cause the most damage are here." Jano began to point to various points upon the body on the floor.

"*Chi* also flows through different points at different times of day. So for a technique to produce the required effect we must use the technique at a particular time of day to a particular point on the body. However, the real skill comes not from knowing the technique, it's about knowing which part of the body to strike at a particular part of the day."

Chojiro nodded in understanding. That meant there is more than one striking point for the *dim mak*. He thought on with renewed admiration to Master Ku Sanku. He understood how potent this knowledge could be. In fact, the more Chojiro knew about the things happening to and around him, the more hardened his view became towards protecting this secret so that only a select few knew the truth. A thought occurred to him about it now: *he knew the truth!* It excited him, but just as quickly as that thought occurred to him, another voice returned: *you must protect that truth!*

Chojiro understood his place in the scheme of things. He went to sleep that night with his mind buzzing about everything he must do and will do in just a few short days. The next morning they set off on their travels again and within a few hours they were looking upon the entrance of the great temple of Henan. They had arrived.

"How long do we have before we meet our enemy?" asked Chojiro as he looked at the temple.

"Seven days at the most," Jano answered.

"Come, we had better get started. The sooner we talk to the monks about our plans, the sooner we can prepare our defence of this temple."

With that, Chojiro led the way.

Chapter 18

At Leon's house, he was explaining the story of what had happened to him over the past few hours. He told of how Susan had shot the two police officers and forced himself at gunpoint in to the boot of the spare car in the garage. He then recited the torture he suffered at the hands of the man now tied up in his living room with them.

"How do you know he's Yakuza?" asked Victor.

"Because he is openly wearing his gang pin," answered Leon.

"A gang pin? The guy was displaying his criminal associations?"

"Yes Victor. The Yakuza are not like organised crime syndicates here in the UK or America who try to avoid the gaze of the public. In Japan it is an open secret. The gangs have offices which can be found in phone books. They also have insignia and they even produce their own newsletters for members. Japanese mobsters also have large political connections which are also openly admitted. In fact, late last century, the Yakuza still had a hand in deciding the eventual Japanese Prime Minister," Leon explained.

Victor shook his head. This changed everything he knew about Japan.

"I thought the Japanese where an honest set of people. Crime is low over there."

"No, their ideals are different. The Yakuza see themselves as modern day Robin Hood characters and the public have an attitude of see no evil, hear no evil. Even the authorities think it is not a big deal to systematically asset strip a company on the stock market. During my research, there was the case of one Yakuza member who literally fleeced billions of pounds from banks in the form of loans. These loans where never repaid and one bank went under from the strain of servicing that debt and the man involved received a five year sentence which was suspended. He is still working on the stock market today, only with legitimate partners."

Victor whistled and shook his head. "So this man here was probably in the business of acquisitions."

"Exactly."

"You mean he would only be looking at the business side of getting the Bubishi?" interrupted Ken.

"Sure. The document would be subject to several people bidding to get their hands on it. The Yakuza gang he works for will probably play everybody off on each other, therefore securing the best price possible for themselves."

"All very interesting, Leon," interjected Sarah, "but how does this help us here?"

"The fact is this man is in territory very foreign to him," began Leon, "he would have to enlist help to overcome these cultural differences and have contacts with people who would be useful to him and his group."

"Which was where Susan came in," said Victor, "I can't believe I didn't see it!"

"Don't worry," comforted Ken as he laid a hand on his shoulder, "none of us saw it and we're supposed to be the experts."

"The problem we have now is how do we get to Susan?" Victor stated.

"We draw her out."

Victor and Ken looked puzzled at each other before returning their glances back to Leon.

"I'm prepared to bet this was her idea. She will want to get the Bubishi for her employers to prove that she is worth her employment with a traditionally patriarchal system before she loses a digit."

This time only Victor looked puzzled. Ken explained this time.

"When a Yakuza has done something to dishonour their boss, the price of such an indiscretion is to present a severed part of their finger. The boss usually preserves it and stores it in their office to serve as a reminder to his employees to do their jobs to his satisfaction."

"As you can see, I suffered the displeasure of the Yakuza, but Susan will want to pave a way for her *sisters*," smiled Leon grimly, holding up his bandaged hand.

"You should get that checked out, I'll organise someone to come over and look at it for you," Victor suggested.

"Thanks. It's throbbing like you would not believe. Right, what's the plan of action? This might be my idea but I can't conceive a plan for this."

Victor thought for a moment.

"Susan cannot think we are on to her. So, tomorrow I'll go in to work as normal. When I've been there an hour or so, Ken will phone saying he has been contacted by someone demanding the Bubishi for the safe return of Leon. Meanwhile, Leon will make good use of the gun he his holding to force our friend here to say the right thing."

"How do you mean?" came the question.

"I will obviously have to tell Susan. I'm prepared to bet she will contact him to find out what is going on. He needs to play along and say the right things, we have the Bubishi hidden at the police station so anything else he says is a bonus."

Leon looked dangerously at the bound man in the room. A little payback was coming.

"No problem. When I'm ready, hand me the gun, Sarah."

"While I remember, Leon," Victor handled two familiar looking boxes, "I think it's prudent to remove these from danger. I suggest Ken puts his safe to good use for the time being."

"No Victor, We need to keep this as realistic as possible. I know it's a risk but I want you to put them back in your locker," explained Leon.

To his credit, Victor didn't argue.

For the next hour the three of them sat round the kitchen table concocting their plan while Sarah remained in the living room keeping guard over the prisoner. When they had finished their discussions, Victor and Ken bid their goodbyes and Leon secured Jirocho to the radiator pipes with a pair of handcuffs given to him by Victor.

Despite everything that had happened, Leon couldn't sleep, so he allowed Sarah to take most of the hours on offer while he stayed with their captive. Because of this a conversation was struck through the night.

"Why did you do this?" Leon asked.

"The Yakuza rescued me from a hellish life. I am that rarity of people in Japan who are frowned upon even in today's modern society there; I'm half-caste," replied Jirocho to Leon's look of confusion.

"That's fair enough, but I'm referring to you. Why are you pursuing this so far away from your home?"

"Because it is my life's work. It is my specialist knowledge that has helped me get this far."

A thought came to Leon.

"Are you a Buddhist?" he asked.

"I am."

"What's the name of your hotmail account?"

"Very good, Mr. Rhodes. You are beginning to make a connection but I am not this particular person. However, the one you are referring to is somebody I never managed to find although I have tried. I have been in contact with them and as far as I know, so have you," explained Jirocho.

"Friend of Daruma!" exclaimed Leon

Jirocho nodded.

"Good. This person you wish to find will help put an end to it once and for all. I never wished to harm you or your friends more than needed. Once I had the Bubishi, I knew to contact this person for their location. From there the Bubishi would have been made very safe once again. However, you were so very stubborn..." Jirocho's voice trailed off.

Leon looked upon his captive rather sourly. He wasn't sure that Jirocho had never meant to harm him. Several sore ribs, a finger missing its top knuckle and nearly being blown up in a taxi made Leon very wary. However, he had only ever considered Jirocho as an enemy. It hadn't occurred to him that Jirocho is trapped in the same predicament as himself.

"How do you view the Bubishi?" Leon asked

"I realise it as an historical document which should be returned to Okinawa. Despite what you may think, I joined with the Yakuza because they were the best placed and financed people to help me find it again."

Leon was surprised at how well spoken and intellectual Jirocho was. He really was starting to change his thoughts about him.

"You mean you were going to double cross the Yakuza?"

"Sure, but in a good way," a smile formed around Jirocho's mouth.

"That is not something I would recommend."

"I know, Mr Rhodes. But after everything that has happened in my life, I no longer care about my personal safety. The fact that I am sitting here and talking to you has put my life in considerable danger. The Yakuza gang I work for will already know I am incarcerated and talking to you, although they have no proof of what I am saying. If you were to let me go now, I would be lucky to last out until tomorrow. My concern is the safety of the documents you hold, this I will help you with."

Leon looked at his captive, unable to believe what had just been said. On the other hand, he knew full well that the Yakuza will have monitored Jirocho's movements at all times. Despite all this he still wasn't sure of Jirocho's motives. He would not put it past the Yakuza to use this as an excuse to get even closer to the Bubishi.

"How can I be sure that you are telling me the truth?"

"Look out your window, Mr Rhodes."

Leon did as he was asked.

"Are there any people hanging around?"

Leon looked out to see somebody leant against the lamppost. They made no attempt to hide the fact that they were watching his house. The minute Leon poked his head in between his curtains the figure waved then returned to smoking their cigarette. Leon noted the time: it was nearly two AM.

"Very early to be hanging around street lamps, don't you think?"

"Precisely, Mr Rhodes. I don't suppose you have any rope to help him?"

Leon chuckled. Despite this man chopping part of his finger off and possibly breaking a few of his ribs, he was beginning to like him and he knew he shouldn't. He thought the same way as himself and the best thing of all was that he knew precisely what Leon was thinking about getting rid of this Yakuza member watching them.

"One thing though. If we are to work together, can you call me Leon?"

"Sure, the name given to me by my Yakuza family is Jirocho. I don't remember the name my parents gave me and I don't use the name my adoptive parents gave me for their safety."

Leon continued to smile at Jirocho. He really didn't know how best to reply to that last statement.

* * * * * * * * * * * *

Jirocho and Sarah walked up to the man waiting under the light of the street lamp. The gun in his hand was nestled neatly in her ribs and while Sarah was wearing a look of concern, Jirocho had one of genuine menace. All this added to an apparently real scene to the man as they walked towards him.

"You look bad, man," said the lookout, in Japanese.

"After what I have just been through, you would understand," was Jirocho's reply.

"What do you mean?"

"That Leon is a nasty piece of work. First he tied me up and used live electrical wires on me then he got his wife to use a little gentler persuasion on me to find out what I know about this document we are following. I mean, look at her, she's nearly nine months pregnant!"

"Where is he now?" said Jirocho's friend with a look of disgust about what happened.

Jirocho jerked his thumb back towards the house, "He's in there. I made sure that he joined their national grid."

The guy sniggered.

"His wife is our guest. She has just lost her husband, so you are to treat her with respect, you understand."

"Sure, I'll find her a hotel room then organise the clean up of the house," he threw his cigarette on the floor, stood on it and went to put his arm around Sarah.

"Good. One last thing," said Jirocho as he pointed down to their feet.

The guy looked down to see a rope snaked round his ankle. He didn't see the hand that had put it there but instead he followed it up to where it was snaked around the top of the lamppost. He looked over to the other side of the post to see a familiar man he thought was dead pull on the end of the rope. With a jerk he fell to the floor banging his head on the pavement as he started to feel his feet move in an upward direction. All of a sudden he found himself looking at the world upside down and with a throbbing pain from the gash on his forehead and all his money, cigarettes and his mobile phone falling from his pockets.

Leon tied the end of the rope to the lamppost to prevent it from coming loose and dropping the guy down. He then bent over to pick up the mobile phone before pocketing it. He looked up at his handiwork adding, "I'd never had thought those two weeks yachting in France would have come in so useful!"

Jirocho smiled. He knew he had now signed his own death warrant. There really was only one way for him now to remain alive and that was to defeat Susan and her Yakuza backers, secure the Bubishi and disappear before they could get to him. He knew it would be difficult, but there was someone waiting for him in China who would provide all the motivation he needed. One last deed then it would be all over, one way or another.

Leon meanwhile, was still undecided about Jirocho's motives. Despite the evidence before his very own eyes, what Jirocho had subjected him to in that dilapidated building only a few hours ago would not leave his memory so soon. He vowed to keep a close eye on him at all times.

Sarah looked at the two men next to her and grew uncomfortable. It wasn't just the unborn child in her stomach that made this feeling; it was the bond that was developing between them both. They were united in something and Sarah wasn't sure if this would end in something bad for one of them. She hoped with every fibre in her body that if anything happened to them, the person to walk away from this would be Leon.

Chapter 19

The plans to make the temple safe against a siege had been finished days ago. The trenches and the fortifications had been put into place. The monks had been very helpful in turning the temple into a fortress and had chopped down trees to make the walls and had gone out to acquire as much food and water as they could hold in the camp. The amassed people inside the temple were now sat around, meditating or practicing fighting moves. Chojiro was one of those people who had chosen to sit down. He had opened the box containing the Bubishi and set about reading its contents and making some sense of it. Most of it was about strategies against opponents and some herbal medicines and tinctures to treat wounds and injuries. However, he was to become engrossed when he reached the subjects involving *Chi* and the Dim Mak. After a break in his reading, Chojiro had approached Jano to borrow his copy of Master Ku Sanku's book of predictions, which he readily agreed to. When he asked why, Chojiro replied that he wanted to use it to make connections between the Bubishi and the Masters book which might come in handy for their battle.

Chojiro spent most of the night deep in research with the two books and only lay his head down to sleep once he saw the light starting to come back up again to signal the morning. He kept himself locked away for nearly two days checking for any discrepancies or similarities between the two books. His eyes struggled to focus in the dim light he had to work with but when he reached the end of the Bubishi, he ran out of ideas and started to look in the box. To his amazement he found the silk lining came away from the edge of the box nearest the hinge to reveal a little pocket. He put his forefinger and thumb inside and found a single sheet of paper which was not attached to the rest of the book. For some reason, this intrigued Chojiro. He looked it up and down to see a flowing script on it which was not the same as the Bubishi. It looked exactly like the writing in the Book of Predictions and this caught his attention more than anything. He looked on the other side to see if there was anything else scribed on it. When he was satisfied there was nothing else, he began to read. It was clear this was in the hand of Master Ku Sanku. The words upon it where of a devastating consequence to all they were trying to achieve. Chojiro needed to tell them all at once. He replaced the boxes into the hiding hole underneath the main building they had agreed would be its hiding place during the battle and he rushed to find his friends. All of a sudden there was a cry from the top of one of the buildings. Chojiro looked up to see where the cry had come from to discover a monk pointing in a westerly direction. Chojiro walked over to the border of the temple and climbed to the top of the wall. He saw a small army coming their way. At the head of it was a man who was very familiar and Chojiro was not surprised to see him there. The person riding at his side was someone else familiar to him. He was, however, very surprised to see this person here. Chojiro forgot all about what he had read earlier and called for his friends to stand by him. All other thoughts left him and he started to concentrate on the task that was now to hand. The battle was about to begin.

* * * * * * * * * * * *

Lord Shimazu dismounted from his horse and walked to the wall of the temple. He stood and surveyed the scene. As he was about to walk forward, Chojiro stood up with a bow and arrow in his hand. He took aim, fired and the arrow shot in to the ground mere inches from Shimazu's feet. Shimazu looked up and smiled at Chojiro.

"You will not come any nearer!" bellowed Chojiro.

"On whose authority?" Shimazu enquired.

"The authority of the people who rightfully protect what you seek!" countered Chojiro.

"We shall see who rightfully protects it!" Shimazu turned and walked back to the line of waiting Samurai. Once he had mounted his horse he swung away from the temple and the others did so too.

Chojiro watched them until they disappeared. Kosaku, Gogen and Jano had watched crouched, hidden next to him and had stood once they felt it safe to do so. Too soon and they would have betrayed their numbers in the temple. They knew that Shimazu would probably be able to guess accurately how many there was defending the temple but they decided they were not going to confirm it to him and make things easy.

Kosaku looked ashen-faced at what he had just seen, but Gogen had again found his knack of saying what was on everybody's mind.

"Did you see who was with them, Chojiro?" he asked.

"Yes I did, Gogen. I can't understand how she would be with them. It doesn't make any sense whatsoever."

"The daughter of the founder of our brotherhood has betrayed us."

"I know, we'll find out Suki's motives soon enough, I suppose."

The group made their way back to the monks to prepare them. Shimazu's army would get past the wall soon enough and they had to be prepared to fight hand to hand. What Shimazu wasn't ready for was the secret weapon four men had in store for them.

* * * * * * * * * * * * *

Three hours later, Shimazu's army had begun their attacks on the temple. They had gone back into the forest to cut some trees, which they used as ladders. Kosaku, Chojiro, Jano and Gogen had mounted the wall with a select few monks and had pushed them back down when all of a sudden a volley of arrows came raining down on them. Chojiro looked up just in time to see them and he ducked down behind the wall to see them sail over him or go into the wall. He looked along the wall to see the others had done the same. He looked the other way and a monk was not so lucky. He had taken an arrow straight into the throat and was now plummeting to the floor ten feet below. Chojiro had given the order not to replace the men if the worst happened and he looked back to see the monks obeying the order. The plan was to let Shimazu think they were making progress before ambushing them.

"Now!" shouted Chojiro.

"The remaining people on the wall stood up and loosed some arrows of their own. Some caught foot soldiers and some caught horse mounted ones but still they cut the number slightly. To Chojiro's right where the monk had been killed a ladder had been made secure and men were starting to make their way onto the wall. Chojiro reached for a few arrows and sent one straight into the chest of one man, another through the eye and a third straight into the knee. The last man howled in pain and fell forwards off the wall into the awaiting ranks of horses and was quickly trampled by them. Jano looked over the wall to hear the bones of the man crunching under the horse's hooves. He winced as he sat back down again. Chojiro couldn't release anymore arrows as the attackers on the wall were too close now. He put the bow down and moved forward to engage them hand-to-hand.

"Fight!" he commanded.

Everybody else shouldered arms and found the nearest attacker to them. Fierce combat ensued and the defenders took out all their men. Gogen and Chojiro had literally grabbed their man when he wasn't expecting them to and threw him over the wall, Kosaku had knocked his man unconscious and was busy re-arranging him so that he was more comfortable where he had fallen and only Jano was struggling. Chojiro came over to him and jumped up grabbing him from behind swinging round and standing in front of Jano facing his opponent. One punch to the stomach, one kick to the head as the man leant forward holding his midriff and he was thrown over the side of the wall where he fell on a horse who was startled by it, reared, flung the men mounted on it, kicking one and leaving the other trailing in its wake by his foot caught in his reins, as the horse bolted off into the distance.

Shimazu was not happy by the way this battle was going. He raised his hand and shouted. The ladders fell away to be laid at the foot of the wall. The horses retreated to fall into line with Shimazu and the remaining Samurai ran to the horses too. They reached for the bags that had been mounted onto the horses and pulled out what looked like large amounts of cloths. The foot soldiers ran back to the wall and laid the cloth on top of the ladders.

Chojiro looked on before quickly realising what they were doing.

"Arrows! Stop those men setting fire to the wall!" he shouted.

As soon as they started to fire, more arrows were quickly returned and they all had to take cover. The next time Chojiro chanced a look down he could see the flames licking away at the wall they had built. There was nothing else to do but retreat and prepare for hand-to-hand fighting.

Once Chojiro and the others on the wall had returned to ground, he used the time they had until the wall fell to estimate how things had gone.

"They started with an army three times ours," began Jano, "I reckon we may have halved that."

Chojiro nodded in agreement. The odds were still not good, but they were better than when the battle had started.

"Now is the time to use what we have learnt. The monks will hold their own to start off with, but not for long. They are prepared to die for this but they will not kill. The four of us must work quickly to even things out," explained Chojiro.

They turned round to hear a crashing noise. The wall was already starting to fall. The fire had spread along the base of the wall and was working its way up. It had even begun to spread along other parts of the temple as well. One of the buildings near to the wall had smoke coming out of it.

With a huge groaning noise the wall started to fall under its own weight as the fire took its toll on the base. On the other side of the wall, Shimazu held his hand up again and waited. He wanted a clear sight of his enemy first before sending his soldiers into battle. He also wanted to see if his guess about the numbers were correct. As the dust settled from the fallen wall, he began to make out the silhouettes of men on the other side. Shimazu gave a quick appraisal of what he could see and gave a victorious smile. He could see that they out numbered the opposition by at least two men to one. He took one last look at his ranks of men and shouted with all his might for them to engage the enemy.

On the other side of the battlefield, Chojiro looked at the massed ranks of Samurai running towards him and gave a shout of his own. The monks moved forward to start the battle while, Chojiro, Jano,

Gogen and Kosaku started to flank the Samurai. They watched as the battle met in the middle. Two monks jumped up to meet their adversaries. One hit him with flying side kick which knocked the Samurai clean out while the other monk was kicked out of the air. He landed with a thump on the ground, barely having time to react before defending himself from a flurry of blows. He managed to stand back up from the barrage and begin to return the kicks and punches. Chojiro saw that all was expected and realised that himself and the others needed to make their impact soon. He looked at them and saw how nervous they all were, even Jano, which surprised him the most. He pointed in the direction they were to move and joined the battle.

The first Samurai saw Chojiro and issued his war cry to him. He turned to his opponent and waited for him to make the first move. When the Samurai was almost upon him, Chojiro closed his eyes, said on incantation to help him perform the move then relaxed and let his muscle memory take over. When he had finished, the Samurai was over ten feet away in a crumpled heap. He made to stand up, but when he reached his full height, he fell to the floor again, clutching his chest. He writhed around for a little bit more before going rigid. A few more moments and his body went limp, never moving again. The technique worked and Chojiro turned round in triumph at the others. Emboldened by this success, the others moved forward and began to cut the Samurai down as they fought the monks and all of a sudden the battle changed. The Samurai began to retreat and Chojiro could sense the fear in them. He let Kosaku and Gogen continue using the Dim Mak against the Samurai and took a step back to survey the scene before him. Was it him or could he not find Jano? He was not on the battlefield as far as he could see and something was not right. Chojiro made his way round the temple looking for his friend until caution caught the better of him and he made his way to the hiding place of the Bubishi. When he got there, his alarm turned to horror when he saw that the Bubishi had gone. In an ever more panicked mood, he made his way past the building it was supposed to be hidden at and went to the far end of the temple. He could hear voices coming from a building not far away from him. Chojiro could see that the flames from the fire were starting to get at the base of the building. If Jano had chosen to move the Bubishi here it was a poor choice and Chojiro started towards the building in an attempt to tell Jano this very fact. As he got near to the entrance, Chojiro slowed down and just listened to what was being said. Both voices were very familiar and they saddened him as they spoke to each other.

"The battle rages, Suki. Let's make our escape with this now!" It was clearly Jano.

"No. You have not fulfilled destiny. You must win the battle," Suki replied.

"To hell with prophecy. I have you and this! Let's go!"

There was a brief pause. Chojiro decided this was his time to enter. When he did, he was greeted to the sight of Suki and Jano kissing. The sight made him want to run forward and tear their heads off. Despite this, he kept calm and allowed a look of defiance to cross his features when they finally released their embrace and turned towards Chojiro.

"Please Chojiro, you must understand that I would have eventually let you know."

"Let me know what?" replied Chojiro.

"That I was going to remove the Bubishi from the temple."

"For what reason, Jano? Why does Suki have to be involved?"

Jano did not answer. He just stood there looking at Chojiro with Suki at his side.

Suki, however, did not want a debate. She moved towards Chojiro and immediately began to attack him with all her might. She quickly found her knives from her belt and tried to use them on her opponent but with every thrust, cut and swathe of her blade she found she could not get near him. Suki felt herself tire and begin to slow down, so fast and hard was the pace of her attack. Chojiro on the other hand had never lifted an arm in his defence and had simply used his body movement to evade the knife attacks. When he sensed Suki tiring, he grabbed both hands and in one swift move, squeezed at just the right point on her wrists which caused Suki to drop the blades and simultaneously, he moved them behind her back before kicking the backs of her knees. Suki fell with little grace, landing hard on the floor. Chojiro lifted his hand and hit her leaving Suki unconscious. He turned to face his friend.

"Why?" he asked again, moving forwards.

"You wouldn't understand!"

"You led us here, Jano. Why betray everything you have helped to set up?"

"I am the gifted one, not you!"

Chojiro stopped for a second to consider this comment. Jealousy was something he had not considered to be a part of everything today, yet here it was, being as green as it ever could be. He shook his head. It was not that easy.

"You are not the jealous type, Jano."

"The prophecies refer to me, Chojiro. I am the one that carries the Bubishi out as the victor."

"It depends on what battle you are referring to," claimed Chojiro.

Jano thought about what was just said. He needed to get the Bubishi away from Chojiro. It was his. The secret should be trusted to him, only him and no one was going to get in his way. If Chojiro takes one more step forward....

Bang! Jano caught Chojiro right across the head.

"Do not take another step!" Chojiro stopped holding the side of his head, "What do you know Chojiro?"

"Something I have read. Let me ask you something. Do you think the battle is one of strength and who has the largest army or strongest arm? Do you not realise that some battles are fought inside someone's head? There have been more battles fought mentally than those contested physically. Do you not think that Master Ku Sanku was referring to the person who shows the clearest mind, resourcefulness and strength of character has won the battle?"

Jano stood there and laughed. Chojiro really was a dreamer sometimes. All this mind, body and spirit crap. He really bought it at times. No battle is ever won with the clearest mind. Battles are won by the strongest army, the best weapons, larger muscles and harder techniques.

"I see where this is heading now. The destiny of this book lies with the victor between us. We obviously have different philosophies which need be settled once and for all. It's a shame it has come to this."

Before Chojiro could even reply, Jano had picked up a handful of dirt and thrown it at him. He turned and bolted for the open area of the temple where the battle with Shimazu's army was still raging. By the time the men had entered the area, they could both see that things had got a little quieter. There was only sporadic fighting left as the monks mopped up the last pockets of Samurai. Chojiro could see Jano go into one of the buildings near to the fallen wall, unseen by Gogen and Kosaku, who were too busy conducting monks to help finish the last members of the attacking army. Chojiro approached them as they chased the last men away. They turned to see their friend and gave a hearty cheer. He swept aside their celebrations and began to tell them what had happened. They accepted this unexpected turn of events with little persuasion.

"You mean to say that Jano and Suki had set this all up?" asked Gogen.

"Yes. I should have seen the clue when he said he invited you by design. The bells should have rung. However, they should have been going like mad when he taught us the Dim Mak. I just decided I didn't want to hear them. It was safer not to know," replied Chojiro.

"Where is he now?" Kosaku enquired.

"That building over there," Chojiro pointed at the smouldering building, "Suki is over there," he pointed to the far end of the temple, "send some monks to get Suki and we'll settle with Jano."

Kosaku and Gogen did as they were asked and then followed Chojiro over to the building Jano had run into. When they entered, all was quiet. There was no sound of movement.

"It's over, Jano!" exclaimed Gogen.

"Your games are finished!" continued Kosaku.

"Let's end this now!" Chojiro shouted.

From the far end of the building, Jano came out of hiding.

"The Bubishi will never return to Okinawa," he started, "its rightful place is here, you know."

"Its rightful place is with the brotherhood, like Master Ku Sanku instructed us."

"We can't agree anymore, eh Chojiro?"

He shook his head, "No, we can't agree anymore."

Jano moved forward and went to punch Chojiro in the gut. Chojiro saw this ploy easily took a half step back and parried the shot. He countered with two of his own. One got through the guard and caught Jano on the nose, the other was blocked. The combatants eventually locked in some furious battle and neither Kosaku or Gogen dared to interrupt. Instead they scoured the building for the Bubishi. After looking for nearly ten minutes, they found it hidden in an alcove high above them. Gogen wondered how on earth Jano had got it so high. He turned to look at a smashed chair in the corner. Jano must have used it to reach the beams above them then crawl along to put the boxes where they were. The one thing that

Jano hadn't thought of was two people looking for the Bubishi.

Kosaku looked at Chojiro and Jano still battling and caught a look at something in the other corner of the building. There were flames coming from there. The building had caught fire and there was little time to rescue the boxes. Thinking quickly, Kosaku signalled for Gogen to jump up on his shoulders. He reached out to grab the beam and hoisted himself on to it. He moved forward until he reached the alcove but before he could get a firm hold, a foot deliberately stood on his hand. He looked up to Suki smiling down on him with an evil glint in her eye.

Below this scene, a monk had come into the building to attempt to tell the men that Suki had disappeared. He quickly looked around to see that they were fighting amongst themselves. The monk decided that discretion was the better part of valour and backed slowly out of the building.

Suki, meanwhile, was stamping hard on Gogen's foot and the latter was howling in pain.

"Do something Kosaku!"

"What?" he asked.

"Something! Anything!"

By this time, Suki had moved in and put Gogen in a head lock. She was slowly starting to twist his neck to an angle that was clearly not natural. Anymore of this and it would surely break. Kosaku looked around for something to help. A burning rafter came down, narrowly missing Kosaku. He looked up to curse this bit of misfortune when an idea came to him. He picked up the non-burning end and held the other end to the exposed skin of Suki's midriff from where her tunic had risen. After a moment, a scream came from Suki as the burning took its toll, Gogen used this moment of weakness to swing his arm behind him, catching Suki in the face and breaking her nose. As Suki leant back reeling from the pain, Gogen reached across her and grabbed the Bubishi boxes from the alcove. The weight caused Suki to crumple and then fall, dragging Gogen with her. They fell the twelve or thirteen feet to the floor with Gogen landing on top. Suki made a strange noise and shuddered as the life was literally crushed out of her. Gogen rolled over and looked in horror at what had happened while Kosaku dragged him to his feet.

Kosaku called over to the battling Chojiro and held the Bubishi boxes aloft to show they had them. Chojiro took his eye off the battle for a moment and nodded. Jano, meanwhile, took this moment of weakness as his cue and went straight for him. Jano successfully pulled off the Dim Mak on Chojiro leaving him in a heap on the ground while the burning ceiling was starting to crash around him. He looked up at Kosaku and Gogen and slowly shook his head. They remained stood where they were. Jano started to walk toward his vanquished foe and began to speak.

"Power. Both physically and politically is something I have and you never will, Chojiro. In your final moments as you listen to me I hope you remember this little lesson I have taught you. I deserve the Bubishi. It deserves me. Not you Chojiro because I am a leader. To have the Bubishi means you have to command others. The brotherhood is nothing more than an army and I have the leadership, both militarily and in personality, to head that army. On the other hand, we have you Chojiro. What do you stand for? Peace of mind? An organised soul? What you believe in is nothing more than spiritual claptrap and all you have done is follow everything I have told you because you look at nothing more than what is in front of you. Now you are about to die for that just like a soldier dies for their leader. How does that make you feel?"

If he did feel anything, Chojiro didn't say.

"Have you any last words?"

"Yes, read this," as he reached inside his robe and pulled out the document he had found hidden. Jano took it from him and began to read.

"I don't need any clear mind and conscience and any good intention and deed. The Dim Mak will always work for me and I don't believe in treasure hunts. Enjoy the afterlife!" Jano dropped the letter next to Chojiro, got up and started to walk away.

After a few steps he felt something tug on his sleeve. He turned round to see a resurgent Chojiro holding it.

"What? You should be dead!" he exclaimed.

"No, I feel quite alive, thank you!" stated Chojiro.

With that, he returned the Dim Mak and Jano couldn't defend it. He sank to his knees, eyes wide in shock. He managed to move nearer to Suki and put one hand on her shoulder. He reached inside his robe, clutching at his chest as though he was massaging his heart to keep going, but he failed. With a last cough and splutter, Jano fell forward on top of Suki. Chojiro turned away from them and walked back to retrieve the hidden document then made his way to the exit. He stopped by Gogen and Kosaku who just stood there with their mouths agape, not believing what they had witnessed.

"Shall we leave, or are you waiting for the roof to fall on you?" said Chojiro, with a faint smile on his lips.

Kosaku and Gogen followed in silence. As they got about twenty feet away, the roof of the building gave way and fell. The walls were next and the building became nothing more than a burning wreck. The three men looked back, the fire reflecting in their eyes. They remained silent, just looking at the scene before them and then one by one, they turned and walked further away.

It was a few hours later, after the clean up of the temple and its grounds, that Kosaku, Chojiro and Gogen had time to digest what had happened.

"So let me get this right. In the Bubishi's box, there was a letter from Master Ku Sanku stating that there are conditions of use for the Dim Mak," asked Gogen.

Chojiro nodded.

"The letter also said that there is another document in the temple which will help light the path to the poison hand's ultimate safety?" continued Kosaku.

Again, Chojiro nodded.

"Then let's find this document."

They were about to begin the search when they were joined by the monks of the temple. They all looked to have a purpose in mind and surrounded Chojiro and his friends in a circle. Without saying a word, one monk stepped forward and handed Chojiro a scroll. When he had completed his task, he stepped back in to the circle before they all filed away. Chojiro looked at the other two and then at the scroll.

"Well?" asked Gogen and Kosaku, together.

"Uh?"

"What does it say?"

"I'll have a look."

Chojiro unravelled the scroll and began to read. A smile began to form around his mouth.

"Genius. We'll never have a problem like this again," he said.

"Let's have a look then?"

"Show us, Chojiro."

Chojiro thought for a moment before laying the scroll flat out on the floor for Kosaku and Gogen to look at.

It looked like this:-

偶遇緊急、莫帶緊入。逆之則其去而來。即之則其去。在上則翻蝶雙飛。在下則樹木來微妙乎。虎狼之爲。猛虎之威。交手興之訶。在着力慾眼賤抖。剛柔進寬。剛來柔中。柔來剛中。剛剛柔柔身搖腳踏腸起身隨、千門口。規矩進退不可。最情是也。

○解脫法

欲攻竝先打西。　欲踏兩移隨後。　欲轉勾剛柔力。　是拔拇川真裁一。

欲攻他被以天柱。　他倒地熱地膝。　從倒地入他膝。　背拖接天撺拷。

若抱前遇、他陰。　挑我膽拇仙面。　殺舍捉戴他嚨。　臨著身用右搂。

雜著身用蓮踏。　右欲捐右先捎。　腳欲踏手先戳。　翻腸誘襲隨後。

撹子手用石柱。　橫子抽用戟戳。　秦菁捉用無脫。　欲踏我其用撺。

欲踢他其用足。　他鵞低勿用足。　他勢而入於中。　取我下乾地上。

取我上隨地下。　拉我縫那脫甲。　鎖菁喉用大跌。　擺步防架他傷。

手足相隨力氣失。

二〇二

Once they had read it, they decided to put it in the Bubishi boxes. Chojiro removed them from his person and opened the box. To his astonishment, there was nothing in it. Then something dawned on him.

"Oh no."

"What is it Chojiro?"

"Jano had the Bubishi on him."

"I'm sorry. I misheard you. Did you just say that the man now burnt to ash in that rubble over there, had the Bubishi on him when he died," said Gogen.

Chojiro nodded.

"He tried to give it back. He reached inside his robes. If I'd guessed, I would have taken it."

"Great. So everything we have been through these past few weeks was for nothing."

"Not necessarily. We know the Dim Mak and we have the letter on how to hide it properly. The Bubishi can still have a purpose, even if it's not the one it was intended."

"What do you have in mind?" Kosaku asked.

Chojiro explained.

Chapter 20

Victor looked at the clock as he walked in to work the next morning. He could see it was a shade after seven-thirty. Susan was already sat at the desk looking through some report when she glanced up to see him, she gave a quick smile before returning to her reading.

"The wife cook you something nice?" she innocently enquired.

"A curry," began Victor, "but she likes to make the chapattis fresh which was why she asked me to pick up some chapattis flour."

"Ah, I see," nodded Susan in return.

Victor opened his file and began to look for were he finished last night. There was a little tension in the air and Victor could sense it. However, he was not about to start asking questions, so he carried on regardless. Susan also noticed the tension, but had come to the same conclusion as Victor.

The room was beginning to fill up and Susan and Victor where soon discussing the direction of the investigation ready for the morning's briefing. Eventually Victor and Susan stood up.

"Quieten down guy's please," began Susan. The room went quiet as they turned to give them their full attention.

"As you know, we have very few leads on what happened to Leon. What I want to do today is to find out if he had any enemies, people with grudges against him. Could you take charge of that Davies? Work with Susan on that one please." Said Victor to a well dressed young man sat in front of Susan who nodded.

"I, on the other hand, will be going back to the safe house to re-trace our steps and see if we have missed something. The rest of you will work to find Leon. I want no stone unturned. Even if you get a rumour about him I want you all to give it your fullest attention until you can eliminate that line of enquiry. OK? Good. Let's get to work."

The room bustled into life.

In the background the phone rang. Victor checked his watch. If he was not mistaken, this should be the call.

"Vic? Some guy asking to speak to you. Says he knows where Leon is."

The whole room stopped.

"Put him on the loudspeaker please. Hello?"

"Detective Ugiagbe?"

"Yes?"

"Leon Rhodes is safe as long as you do what I ask."

"Really? What proof do I have that Leon is there with you?"

"Vic! Don't give it h..."

"There. Alive, well, and in some cases, kicking."

"What do you want?"

"The Bubishi, for Mr. Rhodes."

"And where do you propose we make this exchange?"

"There is a disused farm building on Crosland Heath. Be there in one hour."

"One slight problem, we don't have the Bubishi."

"I think you do."

The phone clicked off. Susan checked the map and discovered it was the building Jirocho took Leon after his abduction. *'Good! Jirocho has found where it is'*. She then came to a conclusion. *'It's here in the station!'* as she watched Victor make his way out the room.

"Vic! Where are you going?"

"To inform Hadrian of the news."

"I'm coming with you."

"If you must."

The pair of them made their way to Hadrian's office almost running. Victor knocked on the door and entered with Susan close behind. Hadrian was surveying the traffic from his window and turned immediately when Susan and Victor entered.

"This is no routine visit?"

Victor shook his head and Susan just stood there breathing deeply from climbing the stairs fast.

"We've had a phone call from Leon's abductor. He wishes to exchange the Bubishi for Leon's life."

Hadrian paused and closed his eyes. He inhaled deeply before opening them again. It was his way of composing himself before making a big decision that would impact on the lives of many people around him or knew.

"Deal," he said.

Victor looked relieved for a moment, then simply nodded his head.

Susan, however, moved to Hadrian's side and began to talk to him.

"We need to make sure we are guaranteed to get the Bubishi!" All pretence had been dispensed with.

"Susan, too many people have died for this already. The stakes are too high. I've covered these deaths for the time being, but they won't stay quiet for too much longer. We need to plan this properly so that there is a minimum loss of life."

"This is the best chance to do something that will make a difference for us. You're prepared to let it go if the risk is too high?"

"Yes I am Susan, and so should you."

Victor had watched the conversation with relief, followed by concern and then utter bewilderment as they continued. Here were two respected officers talking about people lives as expendable in the grand scheme of their own personal life improvements. Susan rounded on Victor seeing the look of distaste on his face.

"When I started in the police force, I got the respect of the people around me and the members of the public. All I get now is grief, abuse and I'm constantly taken for granted. You know what? I'm tired and John's tired. This is a way for us to make the service a better and more respected body. Think about it."

"I don't want to, Susan."

"Then let me shed some light. Perform the poison hand but stop at the last move and you have the perfect restraint. If the prisoner tried to run, perform the last move and gone. A deterrent to others. Or how does this sound? Riot police using it to stop rioters. Clean, efficient, effective. What more do you want? It's perfect. This could change policing in the twenty first century overnight. Law and order would be restored! No kids hanging around causing mayhem because a police officer has the ability and the deterrent. People feel safe to walk the streets because those who once ran it now live in fear of what could happen to them."

"You're talking about a police state, Susan."

"No I'm not. The only people who would live in fear are those who should. Have you burgled an old person's home? Live in fear because when the police catch up with you, Justice will be meted out. This is about bringing the policing that people want into the modern day."

"This is madness! This is the dark ages all over again!"

"No Victor, this is our future," interrupted Hadrian as he stood up and walked over to Victor with a gun from his desk drawer pointed firmly at him, "this is how things should be."

Victor shook his head and looked up. This didn't make any sense until a light went on inside his head.

"Exactly how much are they paying you for it?"

Hadrian smiled and said nothing. He gave Susan a fleeting look which meant their deception hadn't worked and the pair of them turned towards Victor. He quickly realised that he was being backed into the corner by the other two people in the room.

"He cannot know our secret, Susan," said Hadrian blankly.

"I know, but how are we going to do it?"

"I have an idea. One last thing, Victor. I wasn't lying about our future. It involves me and Susan lying somewhere hot and sunny with a large sum of money in an account of our choosing. I'm tired of all this police crap, I want to think of me now."

He pointed his gun and fired. Victor cowered down expecting to feel a bullet enter him yet felt nothing, just some brick dust against his back. When he looked up, he saw Hadrian's arm arc above him and come down with some force to hit just above his temple.

Everything went black.

* * * * * * * * * * * *

Susan and Hadrian returned to the incident room where Hadrian informed everybody that Victor had been relieved of duty when they discovered a connection between him and Leon's kidnappers. He also went on to explain that Victor had pulled a gun on them and had to be restrained. From now on, they would all conduct this investigation through him until a new superior officer could be appointed. Everybody went back to work.

Susan moved round the incident room and talked to a few people to become members of the team to retrieve Leon. Eventually, when she had spoken to a dozen people, she went back up to Hadrian's office to check on Victor to find him on his haunches, shaking his head. As she walked into the room, she had a look of hatred on her face. Victor looked up and thought that whatever she was going to do, it was probably unpleasant and/or painful.

Susan walked beside Victor and then without warning kicked him viciously in the stomach. It was all Victor could do but to keep the contents of it within him.

"Where is the Bubishi?" she demanded.

Another kick went in.

"Come on, I haven't got all day you know!"

Another kick. Victor groaned.

Another kick. And another. And another.

"Where is this Book, Victor? How many more ribs shall I break before you tell me!"

Another kick. This time Victor vomited all over her shoes and half way up her calves. He took one look at what he had done and he simply laughed. Susan was not amused. She moved closer to Victor and took hold of his hand. She bent it behind his back exposing more of his ribs. Five more swift and heavy kicks came in. The sharp pains almost caused Victor to cry and tears started to roll down his cheeks but he refused to give way. She eventually released him and stopped to pause for breath.

"Come on Victor, just tell me where it is. This book means nothing to you, so why are you defending it?" her tone was less aggressive. She was almost willing Victor to say something as though she was not enjoying it.

Victor said nothing but just looked at Susan. His ribs were painful but he could still move.

"Vic, you have nothing to prove here. Tell me where it is. You'll still have a job when we're gone."

Victor had to admit that he had taken it far enough. Any longer he wouldn't be able to help anymore and things would need his intervention further down the line. He made a decision.

"It's in my locker."

Aaahh! The sweet smell of victory.'

"I know," Susan replied with a saucy smile holding the Bubishi boxes aloft from a bag she had taken off as she entered the room, "I just wanted to check you were telling the truth!"

Victor called her every horrible and derogatory term he could think of until she left the room. He then started to laugh.

When Victor had decided that the coast was clear, he gingerly made his way to Hadrian's desk and entered the code which allowed him a line to an outside phone number. He pulled out a piece of paper from his wallet and dialled quickly.

Leon answered.

"Hello?"

"It's Vic. The bait is laid."

"Good. You OK?"

"Sore ribs, bruised ego, you know the stuff."

"The bigger picture my friend, the bigger picture."

"I know, but it doesn't stop me wanting to really hurt her for what she's done."

"You'll get your chance, don't worry about that, Victor."

"After the number of ribs she may have broken, I hope I get more than one."

"It's a promise. No chance of them knowing you alerted us?"

"No, I haven't used my mobile and they don't know that I know Hadrian's outside line code. Should be safe as houses this phone call!"

"Right then, next stage of the plan, they are within our reach here."

"I hope you're right."

"So do I mate so do I."

As Victor put the phone down, he hoped that the discussions they had were going to be right. He knew the way Susan would react when this happened. The fact that Hadrian was also involved added another variable in a situation that was fraught with things that could go wrong. Still, he would worry about that later. Right now, he needed to get out of this room.

＊　＊　＊　＊　＊　＊　＊　＊　＊　＊　＊　＊　＊

Susan and Hadrian had made their way to a car on the back dock of the police station. They were flanked by the police officers they had talked to in the incident room and were clearly revelling in their own self-importance. They led the delegation of people, then cars, out of the station and headed in the direction of the disused farm building.

Before long they had arrived at the building and were busy doing an overview of the property and the area looking for strengths and weaknesses of their position.

Overall they were ten police officers recruited by Hadrian and Susan, they had fanned out in a standard manner that allowed the best cover, protection and returning firepower as possible. Although it was unusual, Susan had made sure that all the officers were members of the armed squad.

Hadrian thanked his lucky stars that he had met someone who had the forethought to do this job. Although they had been lovers for nearly a year now, she constantly did things that surprised him. He made a mental note that when they had finished here and was safely at home with this document, he was going to thank her in the best possible way. He knew that this meant with the tightest possible knots in the rope that will bind her and with the most restrictive mask he had, but when he was ready, that first point of entry in to her will be its most sweetest, savoured and craved for. He would then move round to enjoy the rest of her before he would be finished and the best bit about it all was she would enjoy it just as much as he would. This was another surprising thing about her. She was almost as depraved as he was, yet she looked three times as innocent. The mere thoughts of what she could be like, stirred something in his trousers and it took all Hadrian's powers of concentration to return to the matter in hand.

Susan looked at her superior officer and lover and saw a look on his face that meant she had done something to please him. She gave a small smile realising she was in for a treat tonight before she returned to the task in front of them.

"Any sign of the kidnapper?" she asked.

Hadrian shook his head.

"Surely, this sort of thing is done on neutral territory?" she asked, turning slowly to look at Hadrian.

He then realised that this might not be as straight forward as initially believed.

"Is it possible this could be a flush out?" he said.

"It doesn't have Victor's style to it?"

"You sure?"

"Yes, Vic always made sure that we have the upper hand to start off with. If he has been working with them, they are not in a good position."

"How is that Susan?"

"You know, for a police officer you can be thick sometimes. We're the police, they are the fugitives. We are doing the chasing and as we all know, being a hostage taker is the last act of a desperate person."

Hadrian smiled. Despite their motives, they could cover it in police glory and nobody would be any wiser. They really had fallen on their feet here.

From the smile of comprehension that Hadrian gave, Susan could see that he had got the point.

"All you have to do is go down there and make the exchange. We have snipers waiting with orders not to kill. However, between you and me, one of them does have an unofficial order to do so. You have to make sure that you rescue Leon and then we secure the building. No arrest, so no questions. We keep the

Bubishi, saying it is evidence and then we remove it and say it was destroyed during the operation," explained Susan.

"You have this all worked out?"

"I certainly do, John."

"Well, let's get started then."

* * * * * * * * * * * *

Back at the police station, Victor had managed to escape from Hadrian's office and had made his way to the incident room where several astonished officers where still working. After initial misgivings about why Victor was there he had convinced them that he was not working for the Yakuza. In fact, it was Hadrian and Susan who were doing so. To further prove his point he lifted his shirt to show his bruised ribs. This had the required effect. Everyone rushed to help Victor, while a few others made for phones to report what had happened.

Victor began to explain everything, starting with an apology for deceiving everyone, but they needed Susan and Hadrian to reveal themselves first. This they had done, spectacularly.

"They have the Bubishi, why don't they just go?" asked one officer.

"Some unfinished business with a former Yakuza employee."

"Chinese Porsche?"

"Yes, this gentleman is helping us now. It's a long story, which I will tell you all but now I must get to Crosland Heath. You, Davies! You're driving!"

"Yes sir!"

"Two of you go up to Hadrian's office and start searching, the rest, start looking at Yakuza activity in this area. What is there? I suspect they'll be none but look anyway. After that, can someone follow up on the review of the surveillance tapes. I suspect two familiar people will walk into that factory."

With that, the two men made their way as quickly as they could to Victor's black Astra, which was awaiting them. They sat in it quickly and the car sped away, with Victor putting the siren on, to clear a path for them.

* * * * * * * * * * * *

Hadrian had begun to walk towards the building, when a familiar Asian man had made his presence known and was holding a gun to Sarah Rhodes, Leon's wife. Her attendance in all this made Hadrian even more wary. Then again, a safer ploy to ensure everyone gets what they want. This would make things a little more interesting.

"Don't move any nearer!"

Hadrian stopped.

"Let me see the Bubishi."

Hadrian removed it from the envelope and Jirocho could see that it was still in its box.

"Leon! Come here!"

A sorry looking Leon came out of the building. He looked beaten and dishevelled. There was a bandage around his right index finger. Hadrian smiled. To Leon it was probably just something to help reassure, but to himself, it confirmed that Leon was an unwitting pawn in the grand scheme of things. People were sometimes so stupid. They think they know what the world is really like and yet, they don't see it, or choose to ignore it, when it really shows its face. Leon was just another person like that. He'll walk away, give his side of the story to the police and then be allowed to live his life in the obscurity he started off with.

Hadrian was too caught up in his thoughts to watch Leon as he walked past him. He was also completely surprised to notice Leon nod towards the Asian man. He quickly released Sarah who returned to the building. Leon turned round and kicked Hadrian on the back of the legs causing him to lose balance. Jirocho then found cover as the police took shots at him from their covered positions.

"Stop firing!" ordered Susan, "Hadrian is there!"

The police officers lowered their arms. They continued to watch from afar. Only one officer allowed his gun to remain cocked and ready to fire while the others returned theirs to the safety position. Susan did not contradict the officer.

Back by the building, full scale hand to hand combat had begun between Hadrian and Jirocho.

Leon was quite surprised to see how well matched they were considering the difference in build between them and he was even more surprised when he saw Susan make her way towards the battling men. He decided that now was the time to enter the fray. At least this should be quick.

Leon confronted Susan who looked surprised and affronted at this.

"Give it up Susan! We're onto you!" he proclaimed.

Susan shook her head.

"Exactly when did you start acting the hero?"

"When I realised there are more important things worth dying for!"

Susan grasped the hint from Leon and with a look in her eye that really told Leon she was going to kill him she came forward to attack

"You jumped up, little prick-"

The sentence was never finished as she attacked Leon with all her might. Each punch and kick reached their target before Leon could block them properly. Each glancing blow took its toll on Leon, who was already injured or tired to start off with. Leon got lower by the sheer force of the attacks and time and again he was forced to back off and give himself breathing room before Susan came back with an attack again. He could not counter at any possible moment. This woman was super human in her strength. Where did it come from? Leon got desperate and looked for a weapon of some sort to use. He found a brick which had fallen from the wall. He held it up quickly and Susan punched it causing her to retract her hand and give it a shake. She stopped briefly before coming back at him. Just as she was about to start again, Leon swung the brick and caught Susan on the side of her temple. She fell to floor in a heap. Leon checked for a pulse and discovered one. His reward for taking out Susan was several gunshots at his feet. Leon scampered out the way behind a wall of the building.

Meanwhile, Jirocho and Hadrian were also having a fierce battle which was evenly matched. One punch went in, then two more in the counter and a kick, elbow to the face, a smart move to the left, a counter punch, attempted knee, jumping front kick. All were expertly defended. If a move got through, a combatant reeled and then recovered quickly before returning to the battle. Neither side was prepared to give one inch. Finally, Hadrian saw a gap and exploited it. Jirocho was always attacking to the head. Even in the kick. It was one dimensional at best. He waited for Jirocho to kick again and in a sweeping move took his legs. As he went down, One, two, three punches helped to make the move to the floor swifter and more painful. While he was down, two kicks to the stomach, one to the groin and then one to the head to finish, meant Jirocho did not get up.

* * * * * * * * * * * * *

In the concealed positions above the building, Victor had made his way to the police officers to begin explaining what was happening. Each of the officers quickly holstered their firearms and returned to their vehicles. Victor counted them to make sure they were all there. Nine.

"How many of you did they bring here?"

"Ten, boss."

"I count nine. Who's missing?"

The officer looked around. Eventually they realised who it was.

"Clough, sir."

"Where was he positioned?" asked Victor.

"He moved over to the far side when they started fighting. The rest of us were told to hold fire."

Victor was already at a full sprint by the time the officer finished his sentence.

* * * * * * * * * * * *

Hadrian looked at Leon as the latter made his way into view. Perhaps he wasn't as stupid as he looks, thought Hadrian. He hunkered down into a classic side on horse riding stance and in true Bruce Lee style, beckoned Leon to bring forth his best.

Leon obliged with a flying side kick, parried by Hadrian who returned with several roundhouse kicks, each hitting a target on Leon. He reeled in pain from the kicks before jumping back in and catching Hadrian with an uppercut and right hook, causing two teeth to fall to the floor. Hadrian spat angrily on the floor in front of Leon before he threw himself forwards and began the most prolonged and vicious attack Leon had ever received. If this wasn't enough, Hadrian took the time out to remove from inside his left sock a small dagger that Leon had difficulty defending against. Time and again it cut him when he blocked. Each cheek took a slicing and then each arm. Leon's shirt was starting to be ripped and torn and even his trousers had rips across each thigh. Leon needed to get rid of this weapon, so he did the only thing he knew. He took a blow from one of Hadrian's round house kicks and went to the floor. Hadrian leapt after him bringing the dagger down with him, aiming to stab Leon right in the face. From here it was child's play to remove the dagger, Leon's superior weight saw that he was able to turn the dagger away from him. Their hands shuddered with the amount of power between them. He eventually pushed up and over and started to crush the breath out of Hadrian by putting him into a classic Judo restraint. He reached over the top and when he forced an extra amount of weight down he coincided it with a grab for the blade in Hadrian's hand. He let out a cry of pain as he did so and Leon threw the dagger away and let the hold he had put Hadrian under begin to take its toll. The struggle became less and less as his ability to breathe diminished. When he was satisfied that Hadrian had no more fight in him, he relinquished his hold. He began to search Hadrian for the Bubishi but he could not initially find it. Eventually, Leon located it in the inside pocket of a jacket Hadrian had put to one side before beginning his battles with Jirocho and Leon.

"You really have no idea what you have done do you?" he said with difficulty at Leon from where laid on the ground.

"I have been given a responsibility to protect something. I'm fulfilling that duty," he replied.

"That document belongs to me," returned Hadrian.

"I don't remember seeing any references to you in Malcolm's Diary. Anyway, the Yakuza reward you was going to get would have helped alleviate those feelings of responsibility, I'm sure."

Hadrian looked down and didn't reply while Leon turned away. It was a feeble argument, from a feeble mind and he took no pleasure in winning that particular battle.

"While you hold that document, there will always be someone out to find you, or a gun trained on you. Give it to me now and you can live in peace!" stated Hadrian.

Leon just turned and stood. He watched as Hadrian lifted the gun he had hidden in the opposite sock to the dagger and aim it at him.

The world went into slow motion as Leon watched Hadrian's chest explode into a fountain of red. Several bullets rained down on him and that made sure he never pulled the trigger.

Leon shut his eyes for a second. When he eventually opened them, He looked up to see where his saviour was and caught the outline of Victor on top of the nearby hill, stood there waving a police standard issue rifle.

Police officers and paramedics started to come down to the building to check on the fallen people. Susan was eventually stood up and led away in handcuffs while Jirocho was put onto a stretcher. He had a breathing mask on and the paramedics looked grave when Leon enquired how he was. Leon decided not to think of his new friend for the time being and went to get Sarah from the building. She had been given instructions to return to the building and not come out until Leon had come to get her. When he entered, he could hear gasps and the occasional sob. Leon ran in and found Sarah on her back panting away and holding her bump. The shock and strain of everything that had gone on had caused her to go into labour.

"Doctor, Paramedic! Help Please!" shouted Leon.

Chapter 21

Three months after the battle of Henan temple

"What do you call these moves, Chojiro," asked the monk.

"It's called a Kata, sir."

"This particular Kata is called..."

"Ku Shanku," finished Chojiro.

The monk grunted his approval before walking away from Kosaku and Gogen who had just finished performing the Kata.

"Get them to tidy up their form. The movements are fine but their stances and techniques require a bit of work."

"I will, sir"

"Very good, my child. You will make an excellent teacher one day."

"Thank you."

The monk strolled away. Gogen and Kosaku were silently exploding into fits of laughter.

"One last thing, Kosaku," they both stopped laughing immediately, "before you go, I would like to see that book of yours one last time. Our studies are important to us, I do not want you to take it back to Okinawa misrepresenting us."

"I will come to you tonight," said Kosaku solemnly

The monk bowed, and then continued back towards the temple.

"How much more of this do we have to do?" asked Gogen.

"Not much more," began Chojiro, "I'm satisfied that the Kata has successfully hidden the Dim Mak or he would have said so. Just one more check for Kosaku's version of the Bubishi and I think we can return to Okinawa and to rebuild the brotherhood and its Dojo. All we have to remember is that only us three and the monks will know the true meaning of what has happened here. I plan to include more people, particularly as we get older, but they must prove themselves worthy of the knowledge. They must journey here and that part is for the monks."

It was another three months later that the three men and a now heavily pregnant Shumi returned to Okinawa. There were many rumours about what happened, particularly as Jano had not returned. All Chojiro would ever say was that he had decided to remain in Henan which was more or less the truth.

The brotherhood of Ku Sanku was slowly rebuilt and every 5 years, the members made a pilgrimage to Henan temple without people realising the true meaning. With every trip, some people would return later than the others. If you were a part of the brotherhood, you would know that this was highly significant and meant that you had attained a certain rank and knowledge within the society. You were respected for it.

As Chojiro grew old with Shumi and watched his children grow up and have children of their own, he never stopped marvelling at the simplicity of his plan. All he had done was follow the wishes of his instructors and he had helped make the secret so much more secure that nobody would ever have to repeat the things he had done all those years ago. Despite this, people would constantly petition him to show the Bubishi. As guardian of the book, sometimes he would, sometimes he wouldn't. He liked to keep the mystery and it also had the added bonus of leading people down the wrong path if he wanted them to. As he said all those years earlier outside the temple of Henan, you must prove yourself worthy of the knowledge.

Chojiro died Seventy years after his trip to Henan at the age of 92 on the twenty-second of October 1877. He was surrounded by his wife, children and those people from the brotherhood that had proven themselves worthy. His wife Shumi, chose the next guardian of the book from these worthy people as Kosaku and Gogen had died a few years earlier meaning he was the last surviving person of the brotherhood who undertook the original journey. His final thought as the bright lights came towards him was, *there you go, I did as you asked.*

The funny thing was, with his heart beating its last, final beat, he could have sworn he heard Takahara in the background saying '*Yes, you did. Well done Chojiro, well done.*'

Chapter 22

Heathrow airport was busy as usual when Leon, Victor, Ken and Jirocho walked along the corridor leading to the gate that represented a flight to China. Jirocho had to use a pair of crutches to help him along but otherwise everybody appeared to be smiling and happy.

"Congratulations on the birth of your son," began Jirocho.

"Thank you, Sarah should be out of hospital tomorrow," replied Leon.

"The appropriate phrase here is go and wet the baby's head then," Jirocho returned.

They all laughed.

"Don't worry, he will," interjected Ken.

"Go get your flight," ordered Victor.

"I will, thank you."

Instead of going to the gate to board his plane, Jirocho stepped in front of Leon and went down on his knees. He fell forward again and began to say something.

"I humbly request that you forgive me for the way that I conducted myself."

"Jirocho, you don't need to do this," replied Leon. People were starting to look in their direction at this odd sight.

"Yes I do, I behaved in a most unseemly manner towards somebody I now consider a friend."

Leon stopped for a second and thought. He was still uncomfortable with what Jirocho had done to him and was unsure whether it was genuine that he felt remorse. However, seeing him like this made Leon realise that perhaps there was a good person under everything and it needed an act of kindness to help release Jirocho from the circle of hate, death and violence he was in.

"Jirocho of Shimazu, I forgive you. Now stand my friend and catch your bloody flight. I will be in touch soon."

Leon held out a hand and picked Jirocho up. The pair of them looked each other in the eye before they both laughed and clapped each other on the back. They all watched as Jirocho turned and made his way through the gate, disappearing from view.

"I hope that's the last time I see him," Ken stated.

Leon simply smiled as he led his friends to the hotel at the airport and ordered the first round at the bar. He secretly hoped to see him again but wasn't sure.

It wasn't until the next day that Leon was able to sit down in front of the computer to do some research for his book. He had his son, Callum, in his arms soundly asleep for once and had thought it was a good time as any to start looking on the internet as he had been itching to go after discovering all this new information when the Bubishi passed into his possession. The computer started up as normal and he logged on. His messenger was the first program to load, as it always was, showing his friends and who was on their computer at that moment. To Leon's surprise, it was showing 'friend of Daruma' on line. Almost immediately a message popped up on his screen.

"Congratulations, Leon."

"Thanks. What for?" typed Leon.

"Becoming the next guardian."

"Guardian of what?"

"The Bubishi."

"It's mine now?"

"Yes, Leon. It is yours."

"What do I do with it?"

"You learn from it?"

"Learn what? I already know most of what is inside it."

"There is one more bit. Malcolm left you a page."

"A copy of one. I no longer have it though."

"The actual page is in the box. This is the real secret. I also believe you are good at Ku Shanku?"

"Yes, I won a competition with it."

"Then you have completed the first part of your task."

"What does a Kata have to do with all this?"

"You will find out soon enough. You must journey to see us. This is the next stage of your training."

"Where are you?"

"You'll see. Contact me when you receive some post."

With that, his friend went off line.

Leon waited a few days when finally some post arrived addressed to him. When he opened it, there was a letter saying a seat had been booked for him to fly to Zhengzhou Xinzheng international airport in China. Leon was travelling to Henan Province and if he didn't know better, there was a certain Buddhist temple there.

More importantly, a good friend lives in China.

Printed in Great Britain
by Amazon

21463976R00144